y did you tell him you didn't have a
He stopped pacing and stood in
of her.

ted her lips to the side and stared up at him
bly. "Um…because I don't."

d her to him, his chest still heaving up and
th anger from the guy touching Syd and calling
name.

did you come with?" he whispered on her lips
clenched teeth.

ked her lower lip, her eyes shooting off the fervor
ged to see. "You," she said breathlessly. "I came
ou."

ptured his lips with hers, kissing him deeply as her
unleashed an untamed dance on his. He pulled
the hips and meshed her body against his, causing
rrs to erupt from her throat. Stumbling them back
the wall, she ran her hands through his dark curly
nd down to his face as their kissing intensified. No
man had ever rocked him like this. He'd never craved
a woman, but Sydney was like no other woman he'd
met.

Dear Reader,

I had an amazing ride while writing Sydney Chase and Bryce Monroe's road to forever in *Journey to Seduction*. Sydney is a laid-back woman who prefers jeans, a leather jacket and her beloved pink Harley motorcycle. However, she can easily shed her tough-cookie exterior, slip on a cocktail dress and strut in her stilettos. The only thing that annoys her is her brother-in-law's ruggedly handsome yet spoiled brother.

Bryce loves the banter between him and Sydney, for she has a blaze in her eyes that he finds intriguing, especially considering it only appears when her glare is on him. When they argue, Bryce figures if he kisses her luscious lips, then maybe she'll be quiet for once and realize he's not all that she perceives him to be.

I hope you enjoy reading Sydney and Bryce's journey to love. Feel free to contact me at candaceshaw.net.

Always,

Candace Shaw

JOURNEY *to* SEDUCTION

CANDACE SHAW

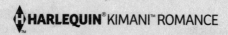
HARLEQUIN® KIMANI™ ROMANCE

ISBN-13: 978-0-373-86392-1

Journey to Seduction

Copyright © 2015 by Carmen S. Jones

Printed in U.S.A.

Candace Shaw was born and raised under the sunny skies of northwest Florida and knew she wanted to become a writer after reading *Little Women* in fourth grade. After graduating from the University of West Florida with a degree in elementary education, Candace began teaching and put her dream of becoming a writer on hold, until one summer vacation she started writing again and hasn't stopped.

When Candace is not writing or researching for a book, she's reading, shopping, learning how to cook a new dish or spending time with her loving husband and their loyal, overprotective Weimaraner, Ali. She is currently working on her next fun, flirty and sexy romance novel.

You can contact Candace on her website at candaceshaw.net, on Facebook at facebook.com/authorcandaceshaw or you can Tweet her at twitter.com/candace_shaw.

Books by Candace Shaw

Harlequin Kimani Romance

Her Perfect Candidate
Journey to Seduction

Visit the Author Profile page
at Harlequin.com for more titles

Acknowledgments

Thank you to the ladies of
Building Relationships Around Books book club!
You ladies rock!

Chapter 1

"Anyone have any pain killers?" Sydney Chase asked the five other agents on her team of the Georgia Bureau of Investigation that sat around the conference room table. "I feel a headache coming on." Actually, she felt light-headed, nauseous, hot and achy. Sydney would've thought she was having pregnancy symptoms if it wasn't for the fact she was single and couldn't even remember the last time she'd had sex. However, she couldn't let the team made up of all men know that she felt like crap.

Once they all responded no, she waved it off and convinced herself that she'd be fine. She tried to place her concentration on her boss, Joseph Mumford, as he munched on a jelly-filled doughnut. They'd just wrapped up a big high-profile case, and Mumford was going around the table giving everyone accolades for a job well done.

"Syd," he began, wearing a huge, fatherly grin, "I'm so proud of your level of expertise on this case. By figuring out the perps weaknesses, we were able to use them against him to bring that sucker down. You're the best criminal profiler this organization has."

Not only was she the best; she was also the youngest at age twenty-nine and the only female in her division.

She wiped the sweat that had formed on her hairline before it could trickle down her brow. "Thanks, Mumford," she said, flashing him a smile as best as she could. "We all did an outstanding job."

Syd glanced at her watch and hoped that he would hurry up and dismiss them. It was one o'clock in the afternoon on a Friday. It was also Valentine's Day. While her only plans were to order a pizza, sip a cool glass of white zinfandel and watch *Breakfast at Tiffany's*, she needed to beat the Atlanta rush hour and dinner traffic. She lived in the downtown area of Decatur, where all the popular restaurants would be overcrowded with couples celebrating a day she couldn't care less about. She wanted to make it home before she sat stuck in traffic. She chastised herself for driving her Mustang that day. She should've ridden her pink Harley so she could've weaved in and out of the cars.

Thirty minutes later, she was grateful to head back to her office to grab her purse and coat so she could skedaddle to the parking lot before the technical analyst—who had a crush on her—asked her out for the hundredth time that day.

When she reached her office, Sydney made a bee-line to the desk drawer to grab her purse but instead she stopped in her tracks. Her heart thumped hard against her chest as if it were being kicked by a dinosaur's foot. The sweat she'd tried to suppress earlier rushed down her brow. She staggered toward her desk chair but stumbled as she reached out for it, falling onto the floor with the chair following. The last sound she heard in the distance was Mumford yelling her name in a panic-stricken tone just as darkness engulfed her.

"Calm down, Megan," Bryce Monroe spoke in a soothing tone to his brother's wife. She was already a fast talker but when she was nervous or overly excited, he couldn't understand her at all. "Now slowly repeat what you said." He tossed his name plate in a box, grabbed it up and strode out of the office doors of Baxter, Clemmons and Strouse for the last time without looking back.

Megan Chase-Monroe took a deep breath. "I just spoke to Syd. She passed out at work from exhaustion and dehydration. She said she's fine, but I'm worried sick. Goodness, I wish I was there, but Steven and I just landed in Hilton Head for Valentine's weekend."

The fear in her voice seeped through the phone, and he had a feeling where this conversation was going. He dreaded the outcome.

"Where's Braxton?" he questioned, wondering why

Megan called him and not their big, overprotective brother.

"He's out of town with his jazz band, and Syd made me promise not to call our parents."

Bryce let out a long sigh. "Where is she?"

"DeKalb Medical Center." He heard a hopeful tone in her response.

"Okay, I'll swing by there on my way home. Will that make you feel better?" He nodded and smiled at a few people who were still in the law firm finishing up important cases, some of which used to belong to him. He couldn't focus on that at the present moment. His sister-in-law was distraught over her twin sister. The twin sister that disliked him… No, wait…hated him.

"Thank you so much, Bryce. I sincerely appreciate this."

He stepped onto the elevator and pushed the ground floor button. "No problem. I'll call you later with an update."

Bryce chuckled. His original plans for the evening were to go home, drink a beer and watch Miami beat whoever they were playing. But this unwelcomed distraction might be just what he needed to get his mind off the fact that he'd just quit his job at one of the top law firms in the country. He'd worked his ass off for the past seven years at the firm, and at age thirty-two, was the youngest junior partner amid men ten years his senior. However, over a month ago, the senior partners had informed him that he would never make it to their position. That was all the ammunition he needed to change his current situation. Shortly thereafter, he'd submitted his two-week notice.

After placing the box into the trunk of his black Mercedes S-65 AMG, he slammed it a little too hard and unloosened his Burberry tie as he thought about his upcoming task. He'd known Sydney Chase for about five years. They ran in the same circles, and, considering he was a criminal defense attorney, some of his clients had been arrested by her division of the GBI. Their conversations were always heated. And she was ruthless. Sydney never backed down during court hearings whenever she was called to the stand to give her opinion as a criminal profiler. However, he rarely lost a case, and she'd often glare at him when the jury would read the not guilty verdicts. He'd wink and offer her his most gracious smile, which always resulted in a huff and an eye roll from her. Then she'd swing her head away from his gaze as her sexy, layered bob cut swooshed across her delicate face.

When his older brother, Steven, married her twin sister a year ago, Bryce tried to be cordial whenever he saw Sydney at family gatherings. She'd ignore him unless the topic was an upcoming case. Their conversations would then become intense, and he sometimes figured if he'd just kiss her luscious lips then maybe she'd be quiet for once. He'd definitely found her attractive when he'd first laid eyes on her across the courtroom some years ago, but her stubbornness and aloofness toward him had changed his mind about ever asking her out. Though there was something about her that still always held his attention. He sometimes looked forward to their heated discussions just to see her cinnamon eyes turn chocolate and the quiver of her lips while she disagreed with him.

For some reason Sydney thought he was a spoiled rich brat even though she didn't think that about Steven. Bryce figured that was probably because his brother was more modest and did a lot for the community. While there was a rumor going around that everything had been handed to them on a silver platter, their father believed in hard work. Despite the fact that the Monroe family was worth millions and considered to be the black Kennedys, Bryce had lived a normal life growing up because of their mother. Claire Monroe, who had come from humble beginnings, refused to raise her children as sheltered, spoiled brats who would look down on those less fortunate.

As Bryce approached the nurses' station, a sign caught his attention that read Immediate Family Only. He figured he'd be fine considering he was Sydney's brother-in-law by way of marriage even though that wasn't considered immediate family. He stroked his goatee and shrugged. *I'll just say she's my sister.*

A young nurse looked up from her paperwork and blinked several times at him wearing a saucy grin. She leaned toward him, resting her elbows on the counter. "May I help you, sir?" she asked in a seductive way as if she wanted to give him a lap dance.

While that would be great considering he was in between girlfriends—the nurse in front of him wasn't his type. She wore way too much makeup for his taste, plus, he preferred women who didn't throw themselves at him—at least not for anything more than a fling. He glanced down at her name tag and stepped back.

"Um…" He cleared his throat and slid his hands in his pants' pockets, "Joan, I'm here to check on my…s… my wife, Sydney. Sydney Chase." *Why the heck did I say that?*

"Humph. All the fine, suited-up ones are taken." She turned toward the hallway to his right and pointed. "She's in room 908. I'll walk with you. I need to check on a patient."

"Thank you."

"Lucky girl," Joan whispered just loud enough for him to hear.

"Me, too. She's…something else." He chuckled sarcastically. Syd was definitely a pistol.

Bryce hadn't seen her since Steven and Megan's one-year anniversary celebration on New Year's Eve. Normally, he'd be in Colorado for his annual ski vacation during that time, but Bryce rarely saw his brother because he was a United States senator and spent a lot of time in Washington, DC. Postponing the trip with his friends wasn't an issue. He believed that family came first no matter what and even though he and Sydney never saw eye to eye, Megan was depending on him.

His thoughts trekked back to the last time he saw Sydney. Bryce remembered gazing at the way her red dress fit her body like a glove and how the red pumps she'd worn showcased her caramel-coated legs. A diamond choker graced her swanlike, elegant neckline and her thick, classy bob bounced when she strutted across the room. Whenever he ran into her at the GBI headquarters to speak with a client, she was usually clad in a pair of jeans, a women's T-shirt that did nothing to hide the six pack that was underneath and a leather jacket. Either way, she was sexy as hell.

When he entered the room, his eyes zoomed immediately onto to Syd as she sat propped up on the bed fussing at another nurse who was checking her IV bag.

"Look, I feel fine. I just need to go home and sleep for the rest of the weekend. That's all. So please remove the IV from my arm," Sydney demanded, holding out her left arm to the nurse, who ignored her.

Nurse Joan stepped inside the room as Bryce leaned on the door analyzing the scene before him. Even hooked up to heart monitors, an IV machine and with a pale face, Sydney still was the little spitfire he was used to dealing with. His eyes scanned the room. A hospital gown lay on the chair with her purse and leather jacket. Apparently, she'd refused to put on the gown because she still wore her usual attire of jeans and a white, low-cut ribbed T-shirt that left just enough room for the heart monitor pads to sit on her upper chest. His eyes traveled a few inches lower as the top of her cleavage jiggled, and he tried to tear his gaze away from the provocative sight. He may not care for her attitude toward him, but he couldn't deny how sexy she was. Her hair rested just below her chin, complemented by her cute pert nose above her pouty lips and her cinnamon, almond-shaped eyes. Even though Sydney and Megan were identical twins, Megan didn't possess the same blaze in her eyes as Sydney did. He hated to admit that was one of the few reasons he actually loved to debate with her. She only seemed to have them with him, though. With others, she was pleasant and just as sweet as Megan.

His cell phone beeped, indicating he had a text message, and Sydney's stare rested on him for the first time. Shock crossed her face as she sized him up with a disdainful expression.

"Your loving husband is here," Joan said in an upbeat manner as she gave a pleasant smile.

"My…?" Sydney stopped as her eyes grew wide as saucers. "What are you doing here and why—"

Bryce dashed into the room and grabbed her to him, imprisoning her lips with his to muffle her protests. He had kissed her deeply at first just so she wouldn't yell out, "He's not my husband." However, when his tongue touched hers, a fervent shiver slammed through him, and he slowed down to savor her juicy lips and their warmth on his. A soft moan erupted from her throat, and he opened his eyes just enough to peer out through the slits to see hers completely closed as she willingly responded to him. Bryce's hand sank into her thick hair, pulling her farther into him as their tongues wound in a kiss so passion-filled that for a moment he forgot they couldn't stand each other. His other hand ran along her smooth arm and down to her jean-clad hip as he clutched it, releasing another moan from her that he muted with his mouth.

Somewhere in the back of his subconscious, he heard the nurses dismiss themselves and shut the door. A forceful jolt pushed him back. When he opened his eyes, he realized Sydney had shoved him off her. Her chest heaved up and down at a fast pace as she wiped his kiss from her mouth.

"Why the hell did you kiss me? I don't even like you!"

A sly smile crossed his face as he ran his tongue along his bottom lip. He stepped toward her and rested his forehead on hers as he stared into her rage-filled eyes that made him want to kiss her all over again.

"You may not, but your lips certainly do."

"Get away from me!"

Sydney stared in utter disbelief at the man who had thankfully backed away and was now leaning on the wall next to the door. She hadn't thought the day could get any worse after she'd passed out at work and found herself waking up in an ambulance with Mumford yelling at the paramedics to save her life. She was glad when he finally left the hospital after she'd convinced him that Megan was on her way. Of course that wasn't true, but Sydney didn't like people fawning over her, and Mumford had dinner reservations with his wife. To look up and see Bryce Monroe in the doorway after he had the audacity to lie and say she was married to him, followed by a long, deep kiss, wasn't how she'd planned to spend her Valentine's Day. Now she was hooked up to machines with an IV drip going through her veins making her extremely cold, even though for some reason she'd warmed up a bit.

Unfortunately, he was right. Her lips willingly responded to his as if it were the most natural thing between them. She was amazed at how his tongue had taken total control over hers in a sensual tango. For a moment she'd forgotten she wasn't fond of Bryce and instead had let him take possession over her mind and her mouth. A tingle between her legs twitched, and she drew her knees to her chest, hoping that would help calm down the sensation.

Sydney sucked in her breath and realized how crazy her thoughts were. Bryce was the last man she'd ever have feelings for, and so she decided it was the medication that was being dripped into her veins making her think foolishly.

"What are you doing here?"

"Megan asked me to check on you. Trust me—if it wasn't for her, I wouldn't be here."

"Okay, but why did that nurse think you were my husband?"

"Because only immediate family are allowed in this area of the hospital, and I know you don't want to alarm your parents."

Bryce was right about that. Her parents weren't happy with her decision to become a GBI agent after graduating from law school and forgoing taking the bar exam. They worried she would get hurt on the job.

While she'd never been hurt, lately she'd felt mentally and physically drained.

"You didn't have to kiss me to prove that we're married. You could've said 'hello, dear' or 'wifey' with a wink or something. I can read body language, you know."

"I think my way was much more fun. Don't you?" His tone was seductive and the sensation between her thighs raced once again.

She smacked her lips and rested her head back on the pillow. "I just need to go home. I had plans." She glanced at the clock on the wall, which read four o'clock on the dot. "Hopefully, the doctor will be here soon with my CT scan results."

He raised his eyebrow. "Hot date tonight?"

She pushed her hair back over her ears. "Yes, with me, myself and I."

A wicked grin etched over his handsome mocha face, and he stroked his goatee. "Mmm…interesting."

"Get your mind out of the gutter. Not that kind of date. I've been working nonstop for two weeks and I'm exhausted. I just wanted to chill on the couch and watch old movies this weekend."

"Exhausted and dehydrated are why you're here. You've been overworking yourself."

"Well, I guess you wouldn't know anything about hard work."

He shook his head, chuckling sarcastically. "Humph…I'm not even going to entertain your comment. You can think whatever you like. You always do anyway."

"Excuse me? What is that supposed to mean?"

Bryce reached into his pocket to retrieve his cell phone. He glanced down at the screen and typed something before sliding it back into his pocket.

"You know exactly what I mean. You've painted this distorted picture of me years ago from rumors about me being a spoiled rich kid that hasn't worked for anything. Yes, my father is a millionaire, and yes, I've benefited from that. However, the truth is you simply don't know me, but there's no point in trying to convince you otherwise."

"Huh." She looked him up and down. "You don't need to convince me of anything."

"Whatever. Once the doctor gets here and lets us know how you are, I'll contact Megan and then I'll leave."

Sydney pointed to the door and almost winced as the IV needle in her wrist pinched her, but she stopped herself. She wasn't going to let him think she couldn't handle pain. "You can leave now. I'll call Megan myself. Besides, what makes you think I want you present when the doctor arrives? My medical condition is a private matter, Counselor."

He chuckled sarcastically. "Because I'm your husband, babe." He winked and sat in the chair next to the bed.

"If I wasn't hooked up to all these freakin' machines, I'd walk out of here right now!" She turned on her side, facing away from him, and pressed the button for the flat-screen television mounted on the wall opposite the bed.

"Trust me. I don't want to be here, either. I'm only here for Megan's peace of mind. She's worried, but I just sent her a text that I'm here and you're in *very* good hands."

Sydney glanced over her shoulder at him with a cold stare, but his eyes didn't meet with hers. Instead, he smiled like a Cheshire cat and his gaze was mesmerized on her butt as he bit his bottom lip. His eyes jerked to hers out of his trance, and she reached to the bottom of the bed to yank the blanket up to the middle of her back. When she glanced at him again, Bryce was arrogantly smiling at her. She turned over with a huff and hoped the doctor would be in soon. Of all the people Megan could've called, why on earth did she call him?

She knows how much I despise this cocky, egotistical, self-centered man.

They watched reruns of *The Cosby Show* in silence except for a few laughs here and there. The nurse came in briefly to check on her and to inform them that the doctor would be in momentarily with the test results. She felt much better than when she arrived. Considering the IV bag was almost empty, perhaps there was no need for another one. Besides, the fact that Bryce was behind her sent uncomfortable prickles along her skin, especially since his woodsy, spicy scent was now embedded on her thanks to his unruly kiss.

A light knock on the door was a sound of relief. She

couldn't stand another minute alone with Bryce. She sat up, and he came over to assist in propping up the pillows behind her back.

"Come in."

An older Caucasian man wearing a white coat and a stethoscope around his neck entered with a small laptop. She glanced at his name sewn onto the lapel and was relieved to see Doctor in front of Smith. Then fear set in and her leg began to tremble as she anxiously waited to hear what Dr. Smith had to say about her test results. What if something was actually wrong with her other than exhaustion and dehydration? She glanced at Bryce, who was still standing by the side of the bed, and instinctively reached out to squeeze his hand. He looked down, gently squeezed her hand back and gave her a comforting smile. But it wasn't one of his cocky, arrogant, wicked smiles that he usually bestowed on her. It was honest and sincere.

"It's going to be alright, Syd," he reassured her, nodding his head before placing his attention back on the doctor.

"Hello, Mr. and Mrs. Chase. I'm Dr. Smith."

Bryce reached out to shake his hand, and she followed his action. When Bryce grabbed her hand once more, interlocking his fingers with hers, she was surprised. She couldn't believe he was really keeping up this charade of being her husband.

"Well, Sydney, looks like you've been a very busy woman lately working around the clock," Dr. Smith began, scrolling through his laptop screen. "According to your medical history, this isn't the first time you've had this issue. Your primary care physician's office sent over your information."

"Yes…I just need some rest."

"I agree, and you need to eat. Your blood sugar is low but everything else is fine. Luckily no concussion when you passed out and your CT scan was negative. However, Mr. Chase, I would closely watch over her during the next twelve hours just to make sure she's fine. Symptoms to watch out for would be headache, vomiting, slurred speech, trouble remembering things, weakness and maybe a seizure, but I don't see any of that happening. If it does, bring her back here. Just make sure she rests and eats something."

"I'll make sure she does."

The doctor typed something on his laptop and glanced up at Bryce with a smile. "It's Valentine's Day, so make her a nice dinner. Spoil her tonight."

"I was just thinking the same thing, Doc. I'll definitely take care of my baby."

Sydney thought surely she'd vomit followed by a seizure just from hearing the conversation between the men in front of her.

"So, I'm free to go, Doc?"

"Yep. In about thirty minutes."

Sydney breathed out a sigh of relief. Now she could get away from Bryce. "Oh. By the way. What kind of medication was in the IV bag?"

"No medication," Dr. Smith answered, glancing up

from his laptop. "Just nutrients to replenish your system."

"Soooooooooo no real medication or anything?"

"Nope."

"Oh." Syd nodded, slowly removing her hand from Bryce's as her palm began to sweat. The doctor and Bryce continued to speak about the checking-out process, but they sounded like the adults on the Charlie Brown cartoons. She was speechless. She'd thought surely she was on some type of drug when Bryce had kissed her and she'd willingly responded—and rather enjoyed it. Why else would she even let him kiss her for so long? Sure, the man apparently knew how to kiss. His tongue had done things with hers that should've been outlawed in the state of Georgia. Heck, every state and country, even. And that was just in one place. She had other regions on her body that wouldn't have minded a tongue journey. When he'd glided his hand sensually down her arm and pulled her by the hair deeper into his mouth, she had the urge to seduce him right then, not caring that nurses were watching their escapade. No. It had to be something in that damn bag to make her hallucinate and think that she could actually kiss Bryce Monroe and enjoy it. Enjoy him to the point of desiring more.

No. No. No. No. No.

Chapter 2

Once Sydney was settled onto the plush leather seat of Bryce's Benz, she knew it was time to escape. Her goal had been to say goodbye to him in the elevator, but the hospital had other plans. She'd tried to protest to the nurse about taking her out in the wheelchair, but apparently it was protocol. Her devoted *husband* had skedaddled out to pull his car around to the patient pick-up area. When they arrived, he'd lifted her up gently from the chair and placed her in the front seat with a knowing gleam before turning around and thanking the nurse for taking good care of her.

Sydney turned to Bryce as he started the car and drove around the winding road toward the parking lot exit.

"Thank you for everything. I sincerely appreciate you coming and checking on me…for Megan."

He glanced at her. "No problem. We're family. So tell me how to get to your place."

"Oh…no… You can just drop me off at the bus stop over on Church Street by the Infiniti dealership." She grabbed her purse from the floor and rummaged through her wallet, searching for her MARTA card. "It's on the left-hand side about one block from here."

"You're not taking the bus to get home."

"It's no problem. I take MARTA sometimes." She found the card and slipped it into the inside pocket of her waist-length leather coat. A dizzy wave overwhelmed her, and she closed her eyes for a second, resting her head on the headrest.

"Yes, but not when you're being released from the hospital."

"I'll be fine," she reassured him, turning her head toward him. "Besides, it will be a madhouse for you to get in and out of the downtown Decatur area with all of the Valentine's Day and normal rush hour traffic, and on a Friday at that."

"I promised Megan to make sure you were fine." His gaze rested on her as she peered at him through the slits of her eyes. "You can barely keep your eyes open as it is."

She sat all the way up and opened her eyes wide, shooting him a glare. "I'm fine. I just need to go to sleep."

"Exactly, and you want to take the bus. Ha! You'd fall asleep and wake up hours later with all of your valuables missing. I'm taking you home." He pushed a button on his navigation system. "Type in your address and then lay the seat back and get some rest."

Clearly, she wasn't going to win this argument, and she wasn't surprised. She'd seen him in action in the courtroom plenty of times. While she may have not always agreed with the outcome, Bryce had always led a very convincing argument.

She typed in her address and pushed the button on the side of the seat to recline it back. "Fine, but only so my sister won't worry." She slid her shades from the top of hair over her eyes and then closed them as she sighed.

Thirty minutes later, Sydney awoke to him shaking her lightly. She opened her eyes to see her Craftsman-style house in front of her and was relieved to be home. Now she could finally take a shower and scrub his scent off her despite the fact that she actually liked the woodsy fragrance.

"Thank you again. I'll let Megan know I'm home."

"You're welcome." He got out and trekked around the car to open her door.

"Thank you. You didn't have to do that."

"No problem." He opened the back door and grabbed a bouquet of a dozen red roses, handing them to her. "While you were snoring, I bought these from a man off of the exit ramp. They were his last bunch. Didn't want the brother out there for too long. It's getting cold out here. So happy Valentine's Day," he said with a smirk.

She inhaled the light fragrance of the petals and rested her eyes on him. "Thank you for the roses, but I don't snore," she said, shaking her head and raking her eyes over him in disdainment.

He choked out a laugh. "Um…like hell you don't. You were calling hogs, cows and sheep. But in your defense, I know you've had a long, exhausting week."

He stepped around to his trunk and pulled out a gym bag. Sydney tilted her head as he began to walk alongside her to the porch.

"You have any dogs?" he asked as she unlocked the red door that Megan had insisted on selecting when she'd remodeled the 1920s bungalow into an updated contemporary-designed home in an upcoming neighborhood outside of Atlanta. Megan and her associates at Chase and Whitmore Designs remodeled Sydney's home last summer for a segment on Megan's decorating show, *The Best Decorated Homes*.

"Um…no. No pets," she said, setting her boot halfway inside the foyer while the rest of her body remained on the porch. "Thank you again."

Raising an eyebrow, he swished his mouth to one side. "Are you trying to get rid of me?"

She pushed the door and opened the alarm panel on the wall to stop the aggravating beeping. "Aren't you leaving?"

"No. Dr. Smith said you need someone to watch over you for the next twelve hours, and I told him I would."

"Wh…wait." She glanced at her watch. It was six-thirty. Was he going to spend the night? "That won't be necessary."

"Even though your CT scans were fine, you just

never know. You could faint again, bump your head and then Megan will kill me for leaving you alone."

A devilish grin formed as she glared up at his six-foot-two frame. "Mmm…" She nodded with a smirk.

"Don't get any ideas, woman."

"Darn it. And to think I was going to fake a swoon."

"Swoon? I take it you watch classic movies and read books like *Little Women* and *Pride and Prejudice*," he said, raising a curious eyebrow.

"Yep, and tonight we're watching Audrey Hepburn and Cary Grant movies until I fall asleep."

"Then I'll be asleep before you," he mumbled.

She faced him, hands on hips with pursed lips. "You're more than welcome to leave."

"Nope. We'll watch your girlie chick flicks. Even though personally I thought you were more into movies like *Bad Boys* and *Beverly Hills Cop*."

"I am, but sometimes I need to escape from my real life and watch something out of my norm like *Breakfast at Tiffany's*."

"I've seen it once with my mom years ago. It's her favorite movie and store. Dad buys her something from there all the time. In fact, so do I," he told her matter-of-factly. "Usually for Mother's Day."

For a moment, she'd forgotten about his rich-boy lifestyle. For just a moment, he was a regular guy, not a millionaire standing on her hardwood floor in her 1,500-square-foot house, wearing an Armani suit and a Ralph Lauren trench coat. Not to mention a watch that probably cost three times more than her yearly salary.

He stared at her intently and stepped closer. She thought surely he was going to kiss her again, but instead, the fire in his eyes was erased, and a relaxed, lazy smile appeared on his face. "I kinda like Cary Grant. He had a certain cool swagger to him."

Bryce tossed his bag on the floor and pulled his overcoat closer to his body. She hadn't been home in almost two days, and she'd forgotten to leave on the heat. Sydney moved to the panel on the opposite wall and slid the thermostat into the on position, setting the heat to a comfortable temperature.

He followed her through the foyer to the living area, and she noticed her mail in a basket on the coffee table. Apparently, the cleaning lady had come that morning, as she always did on Fridays. She sat the roses next to the mail. She'd have to tend to both later. Right now she needed to be alone. Away from him.

"The guestroom is through there." She pointed to a door adjacent to the living area. "It has a full bathroom, and the kitchen is the next room over. Look on the fridge and call the pizza joint around the corner. They will deliver. Put your car in the garage. It's going to be below forty degrees, and I doubt your Benz has ever slept outside. I'm going to take a shower."

Sydney trekked away from him, straight down the hallway on the other side of the living area that led to her office and the master bedroom. She closed the door to her room, flicked on the light switch, threw off her clothes and left them where they'd landed. Grabbing her cordless phone from her nightstand, she dialed her twin's cell phone number.

Megan picked up on the first ring. "Are you home?" she asked with a hurried anxiousness.

"Yes, and thanks to you I have company." Sydney yanked the shower curtain back and turned on the faucet.

"Bryce?" Megan asked, sounding surprised.

"Yes, Bryce," she whispered into the phone. "The man I can't stand is staying here tonight because the doctor said I needed to be watched over for the next twelve hours just in case I have a minor concussion. Even though I don't." Sydney opened the linen closet and snatched a towel and washcloth from the stack. She glanced at her reflection in the vanity mirror to see a condescending expression on her face. *Goodness. Is this how I've been looking at him?*

"Oh…"

"Oh? That's all you have to say? While I'm happy you didn't call Mom and Dad, why couldn't you call Tiffani?" Tiffani Chase-Lake was their first cousin even though she was more like an older sister.

"I thought about that, but KJ has swim class…or is it tae kwon do this evening? I don't know. His schedule is busier than mine, and he's only seven." Megan laughed but stopped abruptly. "I'm sorry, sissy. Just try to suck it up. I really hate for you to be alone, and Bryce is a good guy once you get to know him."

Sydney grabbed her brush and a few hairpins to wrap her hair, laying the phone between her ear and shoulder so she could use both hands. "He's been pleasant and concerned, but more so for your peace of mind."

She thought about their kiss. Their freakin' passionate kiss that sent a shiver through her at the mere thought, but she wasn't going to indulge that information. There was no need. It wouldn't happen again, and she didn't want Megan excited with romantic, whimsical thoughts of something more happening between them.

"That's good. Bryce is very family-oriented."

"I know. I'm going to take a shower and put on some sweats. Bryce is ordering a pizza—I'm starved." Sydney wrapped her hair in a scarf and tucked in a few strays underneath. "I haven't eaten since my coffee and bagel breakfast."

"That's your problem. You forget to eat, and when you do, its junk food from the vending machines at headquarters or some greasy fast-food place nearby. Do you at least have some veggies or salad fixings in the fridge?"

"Yes. I went to the DeKalb's Farmer's Market on Tuesday right before I went in to work. I'll eat some raw carrots and broccoli, dipped in ranch salad dressing of course."

Megan huffed. "Of course," she said sarcastically. "I've heard your shower run long enough. Get in it and don't keep your company waiting."

"Yes, sissy. And don't keep the senator waiting," Sydney answered in a singsong tone.

The sisters laughed and said their goodbyes.

Sydney placed her plastic cap on and hopped into

the shower. It was the ideal temperature, and she let the soothing water cascade down her tired body as she thought about her current situation. The man she loved to hate was in her house to take care of her for the evening. So far she'd done a very good job of keeping him at a safe distance, minus that kiss. She cringed. She had to get that kiss out of her head, but it was no use. Every time she looked at his luscious juicy lips surrounded by that neatly trimmed goatee, she was reminded of how his warmth had engulfed her, how he'd tasted her with tantalizing strokes like an artist's paintbrush. The tiny prickles of his facial hair had rubbed against her skin in a soothing way. She'd never cared for a lot of hair on a man's face, but it suited Bryce, making him even more handsome and charismatic. She'd seen him a few times with it shaven and was never impressed. The hair on his head was low-cut with soft curls even though sometimes he let it grow out into a short, curly fro.

I can't believe this is happening, she thought as she dried off from her refreshing shower. *This has to be a cruel joke. I'm spending Valentine's Day with the man I despise.*

Sydney emerged from her bedroom, relaxed in a pair of GBI gray sweats, to the smell of something quite delicious. It wasn't pizza. Upon entering the living room, her eyes zeroed in on the roses now standing in the vase on the mantel above the lit fireplace. Frowning at the romantic scene, she couldn't remember the last time she'd had flowers in her home. They added a pleasant touch to the room that she barely used. Her nose guided her to the aromas floating from the kitchen. There were chopped red and yellow bell peppers on the cutting board next to the stove along with onions, carrots, broccoli and cauliflower. Bryce stood over a huge frying pan stirring and tossing the rest of the vegetables in.

"You're cooking?" she asked.

He glanced over his shoulder, his eyes roaming over her attire down to her fuzzy pink socks. "Yep. I was going to order pizza but then I looked in the fridge and I saw all of these healthy ingredients. You had some shrimp in the freezer so I thawed them in water."

She stood beside him and inhaled the mixture of the organic vegetables he sautéed. She leaned over the skillet. "Mmm…smells like heaven."

"Thanks. Just need to add the shrimp and the brown rice will be done soon."

"You need some help?"

"You can stir this for a minute or two while I cut the shrimp in half."

"Sure." She scooted in front of him and reached for the cooking fork. His hands grasped her waist, and her breath caught in her throat when he slid his body over hers as he moved over to the shrimp on another cutting board.

"These are some huge shrimp," he said, cutting them in the middle and tossing into a bowl with teriyaki sauce.

Scared to utter a word, she nodded her head in agreement. She couldn't believe she was actually nervous around him. She was a GBI agent who'd interrogated some of the worst kinds of criminals, from drug dealers and gangbangers to serial killers and child molesters. She carried a gun, did karate and could bench press almost half her weight, yet found herself a fumbling mess around him. *This is a first*, she thought.

When his task was complete, she took a huge step back so he could retake his place at the stove, and she wouldn't have to endure his body on hers again.

Sydney opened the refrigerator and grabbed the bottle of white zinfandel that had chilled for five days in anticipation of Friday night. She needed a gulp of it, especially after Bryce's rock-hard body had pressed against hers. Even though it had been a mere innocent second, heat had erupted through her veins at his touch. She didn't know how much longer she could tolerate him being there without wanting what happened at the hospital to transpire again. She couldn't believe her thought process, but she decided to chalk it up to not being intimate with a man in a long while. The kiss had rumbled pent-up desires. That was all. It didn't mean she wanted Bryce. She could barely stand him, even though he was being quite the gentleman at the moment.

"You want a glass of wine?" she asked, heading toward the dining room to retrieve the corkscrew and the wineglasses from the refurbished china cabinet that once belonged to her grandmother.

"Sure. It'll go great with the stir-fry."

Even though this wasn't how she'd planned to spend her Valentine's evening, she decided to make the best of it and to avoid conversations that would lead to their usual arguments—no matter how sexy he looked when he was mad.

"Well?" Bryce asked as he watched Sydney taste the shrimp stir-fry. They were sitting by the fireplace—her on the floor in front of it with her legs tucked underneath and him on the couch facing her. The color in her face was finally returning, and she didn't seem as weak when he'd first arrived at the hospital. But what was still present were her blaze-filled eyes even though they had simmered down.

"This is delicious. I'm rather surprised you know how to cook." She took another bite and moaned, closing her eyes. It was the same moan she'd exhaled when he'd kissed her earlier.

Am I delicious, too?

He sipped his wine and tried not to focus on her tongue as it licked across her lips. But it was no use. She was adorable. Even with her hair wrapped in a scarf, no makeup and oversize sweats, she stirred something in the pit of his stomach.

"Despite what you think of me, I do have some domestic capabilities. No, I don't cook often but I do know how."

"I'm sorry, Bryce. You've been so wonderful to me today, and I keep finding ways to say something crass."

He shrugged. "I'm used to your bantering with me."

"Okay…I tell you what. Tonight, no arguments. We'll avoid any conversations that have to do with our careers—especially cases where you may be representing someone that the GBI arrested."

He laughed. "You don't have to worry about that. Today was my last day at Baxter, Clemmons and Strouse."

She dropped her fork and her jaw to the plate. "They fired you?"

"No. I resigned. I'm in the process of starting my own firm. Something I've been thinking about for a while. When the senior partners told me I'd never make partner with them, I knew it was time for a change."

She shook her head in disbelief. "Are you kidding me? I know we have our disagreements, but you're the best attorney I know. Do they realize how valuable you were to them? Did they try to stop you?"

"Oh, yes. A hefty hourly raise, bonuses, use of the private jet and a company Mercedes, but not senior partnership. I already have use of my family's private jet and I own a Maybach, so nothing they offered impressed me."

"You know, I'm kinda surprised you even worked for them. Why didn't you start your own law firm earlier? You're a Monroe. I doubt you would've had a problem attaining clients."

"I'd thought about it, but sometimes you have to work for someone else in order to obtain the experience you need before branching out on your own. I've learned a lot working there, but I was ready for an advance in my career. There comes a time when you have to move on. When you've outgrown where you are."

Sydney simply nodded her head with a faraway look in her eyes. Bryce noted her wistful expression. He wanted to ask her what it was about, but he didn't want to pry. Besides, they were actually getting along for once. No need to ruin it.

"So have you started looking at office buildings?"

He finished chewing his food before answering her. "Oh, yeah. I have some things in motion. However, I'm going to take a much-needed vacation and go to Vegas next week."

"You like to gamble?"

"No. There's a motorcycle fest going on, so I'm driving up on Wednesday. I go every year."

"That's sounds like fun. Riding one of your bikes?"

"Driving my SUV but hitching the trailer up for my favorite motorcycle or two. You should go."

"Some of us have to work," she teased with a wink and leaned her back against the bottom of the chair next to the fireplace.

"True, but you need a vacation. When was the last time you took one?"

"Um…" She swished her lips to the side. "I…um…"

"You're taking too long to answer," he teased.

"Not since last summer to hang out with my cousins in Memphis."

"Well, I'm sure your brain and body need some relaxation away from work. Otherwise you wouldn't have passed out, and we wouldn't be here eating my shrimp stir-fry."

"Yep. Better than the pizza I was going to order," she said, placing her empty plate on the table and sipping the last of her wine.

"You should seriously think about taking a vacation soon. Just hop on that pink Harley I saw in the garage and ride off somewhere for a few days."

"Perhaps when it gets warmer I will." She stood and gathered their empty plates. "Ready to watch *Breakfast at Tiffany's*?"

"I was hoping you would've forgotten about that." Giving her a playful wink, he rose from the couch and took the dishes away from her. "Tell you what. I'll clean the kitchen, and you start the movie."

A wide, astonished smile crossed her face as she stared up him. "Wow. You cook and clean? I may have to get sick more often." She grabbed the remote for the television and pounced on the couch. "Do you do windows and make up beds, too?"

He chuckled softly, turning on his heel to head toward the kitchen. "Only the ones I've slept in…next to a beautiful woman."

She laughed sarcastically, hurling a toss pillow at his head. "That won't be happening tonight, Counselor."

Twenty minutes later, he strode back into the living room to find the movie on and Sydney curled up on the couch asleep. She wasn't snoring this time, but she was resting soundly. He didn't want to disturb her, so he placed the throw blanket from the back of the couch over her and turned the gas fireplace off.

Retreating to the guest room, which had touches of Megan's decorating expertise written all over it, he removed his workout clothes from his gym bag and took a much-needed shower as his mind perused over the events of the day. They hadn't gone according to plan. The meeting he'd had promptly at nine that morning was supposed to be a final discussion with the senior partners. Instead, it turned into them offering him everything but what he truly wanted. Plus, like he'd told Sydney, it was time to move on. Staying was like being a firefly in a glass jar, making it to the top but bumping his head on the lid and not being able to push through the little air holes.

Then there was Sydney. The last woman on earth he ever imagined he'd spend Valentine's Day with or any other day. He wasn't a romantic and since he wasn't seeing any one particular woman at the moment, he hadn't made plans for the evening. He'd received quite a few texts and voice mails that day and had considered calling one of them around midnight before Megan had interrupted his scrolling through his cell phone. However, he'd enjoyed spending time with Sydney and witnessed a side of her that he'd never experienced firsthand. Sure, she was still a pistol, but being with her today had been a welcome distraction from his life.

After his shower, Bryce ventured back into the living room to find her still sleeping soundly. He didn't want to move her, but she needed to be comfortable in a bed. Her bedroom was on the other side of the house, and while she seemed fine, he didn't feel at ease being so far away from her should something happen.

Sydney shot straight up, squinting her eyes at the sunlight that was streaming through the opened blinds. She wasn't a morning person even though she got up early most mornings. She was never ready to see sunlight until she had a cup of coffee. She glanced at the clock on the nightstand, which read seven-thirty. She slammed back to the bed and pulled the covers up over her head to shield the natural light. Her nose inhaled Bryce's scent and she shot up again, noticing her surroundings for the first time. Black-and-white French country comforter with matching drapes and hot-pink toss pillows. While she was in her home, she wasn't in her bed. She was in the guest room, where she'd told Bryce to sleep. Her eyes scanned the room. His suit and dress shirt were laid across the off-white chaise lounge in the corner and his gym bag sat on the floor next to the door. Slowly, she pivoted her head to the right of the bed and noticed she was alone. But the pillow had an indent and his expensive watch rested on the nightstand.

She pulled the covers back and stepped her bare feet onto the cherry hardwood. She had a habit of throwing off her socks in the middle of the night and was relieved that was all she'd thrown off, for she preferred to sleep in the nude.

The door opened, and Bryce entered with a tray. The scent of hot coffee perked up her senses.

"You look well rested," he said in a chipper voice, setting the tray on the nightstand.

"I am." She reached for the coffee and sipped. It was flavored with hazelnut cream and stimulated her taste buds. "Thank you for the coffee. Um…how did I end up in here…" She paused and glanced at the other side of the bed. "With you?"

"You fell asleep on the couch so I brought you in here. I didn't want to leave you alone just in case you had a seizure or something."

"Oh…thank you."

He'd spoken casually. No stumbling or hesitations. No reason not to believe him.

Sydney eyeballed the Greek yogurt with strawberries along with an omelet and toast. While she wasn't a big breakfast eater, everything looked and smelled scrumptious. She grabbed the bowl of yogurt and sat back against the pillows.

"You slept in here, too?" she asked, stirring the strawberries into the yogurt while waiting impatiently for his answer.

He cleared his throat and slid his hands into his pockets. "I did…but way on the other side of the bed…in my workout clothes," he stuttered bashfully.

Her eyes scanned over his Harvard Law T-shirt and blue sweats.

She nodded her head. His mannerisms displayed it was all innocent so she decided not to press the issue. He was just nervous saying it, and that was understandable. However, that was the only thing she could figure out about him. The kindness he'd bestowed upon her was a mystery.

"Well, I have to get going." He gathered his clothes from the chaise and placed them in his gym bag. "Just relax and take it easy today." He swung the bag over his shoulder and grabbed his keys and cell phone from the dresser.

She slid over to the other side of the bed to grab his watch and reached out to hand it to him. She glanced at it and was surprised to see it was a Movado similar to the one she'd bought for her dad and not an overly expensive watch like she'd expected him to wear.

"Thank you," he said, moving to take it from her hand. He then slid the watch on his wrist. "Remember to just chill out today."

"I promise I will. I have kickboxing in an hour and weight training at noon, which always relaxes me."

"Kickboxing and weight training is relaxing?" he asked with a scrunched brow.

"It relieves stress." She placed the bowl on the night-stand. "I'll walk you out."

She followed him in silence to the garage door. Sydney was never at a loss for words, especially with him, but she didn't know what to say. For some reason she was disappointed he was leaving so early, but she'd taken him away from his life for long enough. It had never occurred to her to find out if he'd made plans on Valentine's Day. She knew he wasn't in a serious relationship only because Megan had mentioned recently that Bryce was juggling women. But that didn't mean he didn't have a date for February 14.

She opened the door and turned to him. "Thank you so much for everything you've done for me. I hope I didn't take you away from any plans you may have had."

He released a heartwarming smile, and her breathing stifled. Had he always smiled like that? She tried to look elsewhere but couldn't tear her eyes from him.

"You're very welcome." He paused as he stepped into the garage and unlocked his car with the remote. "And even if I had plans, I would've canceled them for you. Family first."

"Well, I sincerely appreciate it." She pushed the button to let up the garage door.

He glanced at her motorcycle before opening his car door. "Remember what I said about you needing a vacation."

"I'll keep it in mind."

She watched as he backed out of the garage and into the driveway. He blew the horn as she shut the garage door.

"Yeah, right. When will I have time to take a vacation?"

Chapter 3

Sydney stepped into the empty break room at the GBI headquarters and darted straight to the freshly brewed coffee she had smelled the moment she'd arrived. She poured the piping-hot drink into her oversize mug and inhaled its glorious scent. It was Monday morning, and she was refreshed and ready to get back into the action of work. Her team's debriefing meeting would begin at ten, and it was only a quarter to nine. Normally, she wouldn't be here this early on a Monday, but she'd taken the bus since her Mustang had spent the weekend at headquarters.

Saturday and Sunday, she'd decided to take it easy and rest as Bryce had suggested. Megan had stopped by on Sunday evening after returning from Hilton Head with a basket of healthy snacks and to verify that Sydney was fine. Bryce had even called both days to check on her. She'd kept the conversations brief, citing she was about to step out or take a nap. Whenever she closed her eyes, all she saw was Bryce kissing her, and the best thing to do was to avoid speaking to him or being in his presence so she could get over whatever she thought she felt for him.

She headed to her office armed with her coffee and a Danish. She noticed Mumford's door ajar and stuck her head in.

"Hey." She leaned on the door.

"Chase?" he said startled. "What are you doing here? You didn't get my message yesterday?"

She plopped down in the chair in front of his desk. "Yep, but I don't need a few days off. Besides, I never miss Monday-morning meetings."

"I know, kiddo, but I'm worried about you. The whole team is."

"No need. I'm good." She crossed her jeans-clad legs and tapped her foot in the air. She didn't like the grimace on Mumford's red face. The way he inhaled followed by a quick exhale suggested he was anxious about something.

"Syd…" He leaned toward her. "I've been reviewing your file and noticed you have over a month's worth of vacation leave you haven't taken. It's all paid, but the time expires soon."

She was well aware of the paid vacation time she hadn't taken yet. "No biggie. I'm not going anywhere until maybe this summer." She shifted in her seat.

"Well…I'm going to give you the month off with pay starting right now."

She blinked several times. "What, now? You can't do that."

"I can and I just did." He spoke calmly, settling back in his chair.

"What am I supposed to do with myself for an entire month?"

"Sleep in, hang with your sister or get on your motorcycle and ride absolutely nowhere in particular. I… Syd, you almost gave me a heart attack when I saw you passed out. I know we've been working around the clock lately, and it has caught up to you. It happens to all of us at some point during this career, and it can happen again."

"Who's the profiler you're replacing me with while I'm gone?"

"Watkins."

"Watkins? Really? Then you might as well keep me here. Last summer when I was in Memphis, I swear that kid called me fifty times for advice."

"He looks up to you. He respects your validation."

She sighed and ran her hands through her hair. "Fine. Go ahead and process my vacation paperwork." She stood, unhooked the gun from her holster and set the weapon on his desk.

He patted a folder with a sly smile. "Already did. Now get out of here before I change my mind."

That afternoon, Sydney cuddled on her couch searching the internet for vacation spots while *Bad Boys* played on the flat screen in the background. She couldn't believe she didn't fight harder with Mumford about taking the vacation. This wasn't the first time he'd demanded she take a break, but in the past he'd always lost. She hated to admit that she was looking forward to the month off. Lately, she'd been stressed with the job that she loved and couldn't pinpoint why all of a sudden she found it taxing. However, Bryce's statement—*there comes a time when you have to move on*—had played in her head all weekend. She'd contemplated taking the bar exam just to have it to fall back on. She'd studied for it off and on over the years, but her career had always gotten in the way. Plus, she wasn't sure if that was the side of the law she wanted to be on. That reason alone was why she had decided not to take the bar after law school, much to her parents' dismay.

Sydney continued searching for vacation spots while laughing at Martin Lawrence and Will Smith. The movie was on mute, but she knew the lines by heart. She didn't see anywhere she wanted to go on the spur of the moment, and since it was winter, riding her motorcycle somewhere was out of the question. She thought about the motorcycle fest Bryce had mentioned but couldn't remember the name of it. After reaching for her cell phone, she scrolled through until she saw his name, but she pushed the screen button off instead.

She jumped up from the couch, tossing the phone onto one of the cushions, and headed to the laundry room to check on the towels in the dryer. Fifteen minutes later, she strolled by the couch, glanced at the phone and released a low groan on the way to the linen closet in the hallway. Afterward, she sat on the floor and slid the laptop on her lap to continue searching for a quick getaway even though the trip to Vegas was the only one she was remotely interested in. Her eyes roamed toward the phone, but she shook her head and searched for motorcycle fests in Vegas instead. Nothing came up.

Retreating to the kitchen, she glanced at the pizza place's take-out menu on the refrigerator. Next to it was Bryce's card with all of his contact numbers. *How did that get there?* She moaned and decided against the pizza. A salad with grilled chicken was the better choice.

Thirty minutes later, she plopped back on the couch with her hearty salad and stared straight ahead at the roses on the mantel. Even though Bryce only bought them because they were the seller's last dozen, she couldn't help but love their presence in her home. She glanced at her cell phone again, then back at the flowers.

Sydney still couldn't shake her thoughts of him. Everything from his tantalizing scent to his sexy smile to his charismatic nature burrowed into her brain. The way he kissed her. The way he handled her. She couldn't help but fantasize how he'd be if things ever went any further. His warm, brown skin on hers, caressing and stroking her naked body while bestowing his skillful tongue over every inch of her, sent a shiver of raw pleasure through her veins.

"This can't be happening," she screamed out loud.

"I'm not sitting here thinking about that arrogant, conceited man."

But he'd been none of those things when he'd held her hand tightly in the hospital or when he'd cooked her dinner and made sure nothing happened to her while she slept. The man she knew from the courtroom wasn't the man who took care of her. Who had called her twice to check on her, and gave her roses that were blooming so beautifully and filling her living room with a sweet fragrance.

Sydney glanced at her cell phone again. "Okay. I'm only calling to ask for some information. Not a date."

Bryce strolled confidently out of the meeting with his real-estate broker in the Equitable Building in the downtown Atlanta area. He'd found the perfect location for his law offices in midtown Atlanta and would close in less than a month. Turning the corner on Peachtree Street, he decided to grab some dessert at Café Intermezzo before heading back to his home in Buckhead.

The vibration of his cell phone interrupted his perusal of the menu. The phone had rung all day with business calls, and he really wanted to turn if off, but he needed to get things squared away before he left for Vegas on Wednesday afternoon. A surprised grin etched across his face at the picture of the sleeping beauty that was displayed on his screen. He'd snapped it on a whim and had found himself staring at it every now and then for the past few days. Now seeing it flash on his screen had him curious as to why she was actually calling him.

"Hey, Syd. Everything okay?" He sipped his café au lait and closed the menu, deciding upon a tiramisu cheesecake.

"Everything is fine. I just had a quick question if you aren't busy…"

"Go ahead." He leaned back in his chair. "I'm all ears."

"I just wanted to know the name of the motorcycle fest you mentioned in Vegas. I'm thinking about going if it's not too late, but I can't find it online."

"No, it's not too late." The waitress came back and he opened the menu, pointing to the cheesecake. "I'll text you the information in a moment. It's hosted by a private motorcycle club I belong to for professionals. That's probably why you can't find it. I'll add your name to my guest list and send you the access number you'll need to register." He grabbed his iPad from his briefcase to place her name on his friends and family list.

"Oh, wow. Thank you so much."

"No problem. So you're taking some time off after all?"

"I don't have a choice. My boss gave me a month's leave of absence. It's my built-up vacation time."

"You have that much vacation leave that you haven't taken? It's definitely time for one then. That's what your body has been trying to tell you."

"Well, apparently, everyone but me realized it. I'll

check out the fest and decide if that's somewhere I want to go. I'm looking at a few other places, as well."

He rapidly tapped his finger on the table as his brain worked in overtime. "How about you ride with me? My trailer holds two motorcycles. I'm leaving Wednesday around two in the afternoon. I could use another driver."

"Oh…no. I'll probably fly. I may not even go. I'm just looking at all options."

"Well, let me know if you decide to go. Maybe we can hang out since we're semi–getting along now."

"Um…I'm sure if I go we'll run into each other."

"Yeah…or you can call me," he suggested in a low, sexy voice.

She laughed nervously. "Um…I gotta go…wash this conditioner out of my hair, but please text me the information."

He chuckled silently. He hadn't heard that excuse from a woman in ages.

"Will do, Syd."

"What kind of excuse was that?" Sydney asked herself out loud. "Wash the conditioner out of my hair?" However, the lazy, seductiveness in his voice when he'd said, "Or you can call me," surely had an underlying message. The profiler in her heard it. She even imagined him saying it through his inviting lips that had probably curled into a jaw-dropping, arrogant smirk. If it had been in person, he would've stepped into her personal space and winked. Maybe even licked his lips and pulled her hard against him as he had in the hospital, gripping her hips or maybe her butt this time.

Argh! Why can't I get this man out of my head?

Sydney took a deep breath and opened the website for the festival. While it wasn't too late to attend, the late registration fee was five hundred dollars. The airplane ticket was way too much, so she decided she would have to drive. That way she could hitch up her motorcycle trailer to the back of her Mustang. She'd done it before. No big deal. Sure, it would be a two-day drive, but, heck, she had a month off. What else was she doing? And if she ran into Bryce, so what? She was a tough cookie. She'd dealt with the most wanted criminals for the past five years saying all types of sexist things to her or wagging their tongues at her, among other rude gestures. A few even had the audacity to touch her and had ended up with a broken finger or five. She could handle being around Bryce Monroe.

She grabbed her cell phone to send him a text message.

I've made my reservations. See you in Vegas! Sydney pressed Send and grabbed the remote to finish watching *Bad Boys*.

Perfect. That wasn't so bad. She could be cool with him. While the kiss had been mind-blowing and hot, it didn't mean anything. He was simply trying to keep up with the charade of being her husband. He probably hadn't even given it another thought. Besides, there would be at least a thousand bikers in Las Vegas all clad in black leather. Running into him would be unlikely.

Her phone chimed with a message from him.

I'm staying at the Bellagio. What about you?

Great! Me, too.

Great…me, too. Her jaw tightened as she glared at the roses on the mantel and let out a loud, long sarcastic laugh.

"Darn it!" Sydney slammed her hand on the steering wheel of her seven-year-old Mustang. She exhaled slowly. "It's just cold. That's all." She rubbed the dashboard as her car kept jumping and pulling while she sat at the stop sign in her neighborhood. She'd called the auto shop that she always used that wasn't far from her house and hoped she could make it there. Her bags were packed and her cooler was full of food. The goal was to be on the road by nine so she could drive all day until the sun went down but this was putting a monkey wrench in her plans. Hopefully, whatever was wrong with the car could be fixed and wouldn't cost that much. Though she had an inkling it was the transmission with the way the gears were slipping, and that would cost a pretty penny to fix.

"Three…what? Stan, you gotta be kidding me." The wind had been completely knocked out of her. Three thousand dollars? Sure, she had the money in her savings account, but it was going toward a down payment for a new Mustang. She was hoping her car would last until the end of the year. She glanced at it through the window as she stood in the waiting room of the auto shop.

"I'm afraid so, Syd. Your transmission and the car's computer are failing, not to mention the radiator—"

"Stop. I don't think my heart can take any more."

"However, I can try to find you a used computer and rebuild the transmission all for about half of what I quoted you."

She glanced at her watch. "How long will it take?"

"Today's Wednesday. I can have it ready by Monday. Gotta find a used computer first."

"Okay."

"I'll get one of the mechanics to drive you home."

Once she arrived back home, she immediately looked at rental cars and plane tickets online. She didn't want to fly because she wanted to take her motorcycle, and she hated driving rental cars. She thought about just canceling the trip but the registration fee was final plus she'd entered a few contests including a motorcycle race that she was looking forward to. She rested her head back on her couch as her eyes diverted toward her packed bags and her ice cooler sitting by the garage door. Sighing, she decided she would just rent a car.

Her cell phone chimed and vibrated from her purse sitting on the floor by her feet. She hoped it wasn't Stan calling with more bad news about her car. She glanced at the screen. It was a text from Bryce.

When are you leaving? I'm leaving around ten. My meeting was canceled.

Don't know. My car is in the shop. Going to rent a car.

She was about to send him another text but the phone rang. It was him.

"Hello?"

"Don't rent a car. You can ride with me. There's plenty of room in my Range Rover."

"Bryce...I don't think that's a good idea."

"And driving by yourself for two days is?"

"In case you forgot, I can take care of myself. I have my gun and a Taser, plus I have my black belt in karate."

"Okay...but—"

"Besides, we'll just argue the entire time like we always do."

"We didn't argue the last time we were together. Personally, I think we'll get along just fine. If you get tired of me, just hop in the backseat and watch a movie. You can bring all of your classics."

She sighed. It all sounded so tempting. Plus, she had decided that whatever she thought she felt for Bryce wasn't real.

"Okay. I'll ride with you to Vegas."

"Perfect. See you soon."

Chapter 4

Bryce secured Sydney's motorcycle onto the trailer next to his all-black Harley. He couldn't believe a manly man like himself was going to drive cross-country with a pink motorcycle hitched to the back of his SUV.

He placed the luggage and cooler she'd left in the open garage in the trunk. She still hadn't emerged from the house yet except to stick her head out to say her belongings were by the door.

Looking at the time on his cell phone, Bryce heard the garage door close and Sydney's footsteps on the driveway. He glanced up and almost did a double take. She was delectable in a pair of black shades, a short black sweater dress that hugged her lethal curves and a gold-and-silver twisted belt around her waist. Even though she did weight training and kickboxing to stay in shape for her job and was toned, she still had a dainty figure that didn't fit her personality. He let his eyes peruse down her bare legs to her flat ankle boots.

"Aren't you going to be cold without any type of… panty hose or leggings?" Not that he really cared. She had a pair of muscular, sexy legs that he wouldn't mind being lost in between.

"I tend to get hot while traveling in the car. I have a throw blanket in my tote bag, and your Range does have heat, right?" she asked sarcastically.

He closed the gap between them. "Yes, or you can throw them across my lap."

She twisted her lips into a frustrated smile. "I'll pass. You just concentrate on the road, Counselor."

Moments later they were on the interstate headed toward Tennessee. He tried to keep focused on the road but kept glancing in her direction. He wasn't sure if he should make small talk or not. She seemed content reading a magazine and bopping her head to the music that streamed through the speakers.

"So does your family know you're going to Vegas?" he asked.

"Yep. My mom had a panic attack, and my dad said have fun and to split my winnings with him," she answered. "Braxton didn't question me, but my other half suggested I go somewhere else. She has never fully understood why I love motorcycles."

"Hmm, and why do you love motorcycles?"

"Just the sheer excitement and exhilaration to be in total control of the sleek, sexy machine. It's almost like

great sex but better and without a sweaty man underneath me."

"Better? I don't know about that. Maybe you've been
with the wrong men." He paused and momentarily
glimpsed in her direction. "So you like being in control…and on top?" He tried to contain the wide smile,
but it was no use. The visual he conjured up of her riding him hard while he tightly grasped her fine bottom
sent his mind and his foot on the pedal in overdrive.

"You wanna slow down?" She pointed to the speed-
ometer. He was going eighty-five.

"Oh. Sorry, my mind was somewhere else," he said,
slowing down to a few miles over the speed limit.

"Yeah, like in the gutter. I was talking about riding
a motorcycle, not a man."

"Well, I can see how the two can be similar. For me,
I love the force and the powerful engine underneath. I
love the roar and the exquisite sexy hum when it's idle.
But then you speed up again until you finally reach your
destination… The true destination for me is the after-
math and thrill of being in control and becoming one
with the ride. Sometimes bumpy, sometimes smooth
but overall *quite* satisfying."

Out of the corner of his eye, he saw her cross and un-
cross her legs as a pursed smirk formed, and her cheeks
turned a rosy pink.

"Is that similar to your experiences, Syd?"

"Um…it just depends on my mood." She ran her
fingers through her hair. "Sometimes if I'm stressed, I
ride really, really fast…you know. To get out all of my

frustrations and pent-up energy. Scream at the top of my lungs along with the revved up engine. Then there are times I just want to be lazy and relax. Let the motorcycle drive and guide me and afterward float back down from pure bliss."

It took every fiber in his being not to pull over and snatch her on top of him just to see how fast and passionate she could really ride and drive him, with him in control guiding her how he wanted. How he needed.

She pushed her shades up on her head, and he saw her eyes for the first time since their trip had begun. They'd turned dark cinnamon with a sparkle of fire like always, except this time she wasn't arguing with him, which was what usually provoked her heat-filled eyes. He stroked his goatee. How had he missed it this entire time? She wasn't angry with him. She was turned on by him.

"Well, maybe one day we'll go riding together," he suggested, his voice laced with lust and sex.

"Only if I get to drive one of your bikes."

"Oh, so you know about my collection?"

"I saw them in your garage when you hosted Megan and Steven's engagement party. Megan showed me, thinking we'd have something else to talk about instead of arguing about cases."

"But you've never mentioned them. I knew you had one, but I kinda thought you had a little scooter or something—not a Harley. A pink one…but Harley all the same."

"Mmm…I guess I thought getting along with you

would end our bantering. We're on the opposite sides
of the law. You defend criminals who you clearly know
are guilty. We just don't arrest people without hard evidence. I have to stay true to my beliefs. I couldn't let
my guard down, especially with you."

"But you just did."

She groaned, sliding her shades back over her eyes,
and turned her head toward the window.

Yes, I just had the audacity to let my guard down.
How did a conversation about motorcycles turn into a
sexual, erotic escapade? True, riding a motorcycle was
truly a high like an orgasm, especially since she hadn't
experienced one in who knew how long. Years perhaps.
Even though she'd had sex in the past, she had never experienced an over-the-top, earth-shattering, bed-rocking
orgasm. Syd had just figured they were overrated and
people were lying about having multiple ones in a row.
Even though there'd been the hint of one when Bryce
had kissed her and set off some kind of electric spark.
And a few moments ago when he was describing his
motorcycle experience, it happened again. However, it
had been almost a year since she'd had sex, and apparently her body was tired of the dry spell.

Sydney opened her fashion magazine again, flipping
through expensive clothes, purses and jewelry that she'd
never buy, at least not at those prices. She didn't mind
waiting until the season was over with to shop at the
outlet malls. She glanced at Bryce. He was completely

focusing on the road ahead, but she didn't like a silent, awkward road trip.

"So how old were you when you got your first motorcycle?"

"Eighteen, and it was a little scooter. Nothing fancy. I saved my money from working in the law firm of one of my father's golf buddies the summer before I went to college."

"Wait a minute." She paused, not believing him. "You bought it yourself?"

"Yes…despite what you may think about me, I didn't just have things handed to me on a silver platter from our butlers, Jeffrey and Belvedere. Yes, I had everything I needed, but my father believed in working hard. When I was sixteen and asked for a Mercedes, he laughed at me and bought me a Honda. A used, five-year-old Honda that I was responsible for putting the down payment on. He said if I wanted a Mercedes, I would have to buy it when I graduated from college and got a job."

"You really had butlers named Jeffrey and Belvedere?"

"No." He smiled.

"Oh."

"Their names were Chauncey and Gordon," Bryce answered with a laugh.

"Ha-ha." She punched his shoulder teasingly. "So you were the only kid at your private school with a Honda and everyone else Mercedes and beamers."

"Nope. Wrong again, grasshopper. I went to a public school. Now mind you, it was in a nice neighborhood, so there were still some high-end cars in the student parking lot."

Her eyes rounded, and she swore she needed to get her hearing checked. "You went to a public school?"

"Yep. From kindergarten to twelfth grade. I went to elementary school where my mom taught, like you and your siblings did with your mother."

She smirked, remembering those days. "Right, but at least your dad wasn't your assistant principal in middle school and your uncle your principal in high school."

"No, I was grateful when I went to middle school. It was sort of hard to be mischievous when your mom's classroom was just down the other hallway. I guess you and Megan never got in trouble, either."

"Megan, no. Braxton, sometimes. And me…well…a few times. I got caught smoking a cigarette in the girls' bathroom in eighth grade and my dad suspended me."

He laughed hysterically. "Wow, your dad suspended you? Do you still smoke?"

"No. That was the first and last time. Do you?"

"An occasional cigar. So did you and Megan ever do the twin switch?"

She laughed out loud. "Oh, yes, and one time it backfired really, really bad."

"What happened?"

"Sixth grade, pre-algebra test. I'd taken the test in first period, and I knew I aced it. Megan had the test in third period and was nervous. During that time, our mom was still dressing us exactly alike from our hair ribbons, earrings, fingernail polish. Literally everything. And besides from Braxton and our parents, no one knew who was who. Anyway, I offered to take the test for her, and she went to my English class that she had first period. Well, the assistant principal, i.e., my father, decided to do teacher evaluations that day and walked into Mrs. Snow's math class expecting to see Megan."

"Oh, no!"

"Oh, no is right. I was trying to keep my eyes down-cast on the test. Otherwise he would've known it was me. Dad always says that even though Megan's eyes and mine are shaped the same and are the same color, I have more fire in mine and that's how he tells us apart. Well, he'd barely glanced at me and shouted, "Sydney, what are you doing in here?" I tried to say I was Megan, but there was no point. We both ended up with zeroes on the test, after-school detention, and were grounded for a month. After that, Mother never dressed us ex-actly alike again."

"That was a funny story," he said, chuckling.

"It wasn't funny then."

She yawned and immediately tried to muffle it so he wouldn't yawn, too. She didn't want him to become tired. When she traveled with her family, she was al-ways in charge of keeping her father entertained so he wouldn't get bored and sleepy while driving.

Syd thought about their conversation and was quite surprised to learn that the Monroes had actually attended public school and he'd had to help buy his own car as a teenager. For some reason, she'd always thought Bryce was the flashier one of the two brothers with his mansion in an exclusive neighborhood, motorcycle collection, designer clothes and expensive watches. Steven had always seemed to be the more humble and modest Monroe. In the media, his campaign team had painted him as a down-to-earth guy who didn't care about his millions and only cared about the welfare of his constituents and helping others. Once she'd met him, she'd realized that truly was his character. His only flaw had been his playboy ways, but, thanks to Megan, he had finally settled down.

Now it seemed perhaps she'd been wrong about Bryce. He didn't come across as the spoiled rich brat that she perceived him to be.

"I can drive so you can take a break," she offered, sliding her feet from underneath her and settling them on the floor next to her purse. "You've been driving for three hours straight."

"I'm good, but we can stop at a rest area to stretch for a bit. There's one coming up soon."

"Okay, and we can eat lunch. I brought some things to make sandwiches and some other goodies."

Thirty minutes later they sat at a picnic bench in a sunny spot a few feet away from Bryce's SUV. There were a few other travelers eating or walking their dogs in the area restricted for them.

"I should travel with you more often," Bryce said before biting into his turkey and cheese sandwich. "Reminds me of the times growing up and traveling with my family in our Winnebago. Mom would make sand-wiches, fried chicken, salads and cookies."

"Really? You mean y'all didn't take the private jet?" she asked teasingly, munching on a sweet potato chip.

"Sometimes, but that was more so for Dad's busi-ness travels. For family trips, unless it was overseas or a minivacation, we would drive cross-country. It was more fun that way."

"I know what you mean. So you didn't pack any food for this long trip that you originally were going to take by yourself?"

"Nope. Just some bottled waters and the sweet po-tato chips. I was just going to stop when I got hungry."

"Oh…well, I like to bring food to save money." She stopped as she reminded herself that wasn't a priority of his even though he apparently did know the value of work-ing hard in order to buy his first car and motor scooter.

Sydney's cell phone beeped from inside her purse. She pulled it out to see a text from Megan.

Just checking on you.

I'm fine. At a rest area eating lunch.

Don't drive all night. Just stop over somewhere and get some rest. I hate that you're traveling alone.

Trust me I'll be fine. TTYL

TTYL

Sydney tossed the phone back into her purse and folded her paper plate, setting her empty bottled water on top of it. She grabbed their trash and threw it in the can behind her.

"That was Megan checking on me. She wanted to make sure I was fine."

"Yeah…considering you're with me, she probably thinks we've argued the entire time."

"Oh…actually she doesn't know I'm with you. I haven't spoken to her since before my car had issues. She's shooting scenes for *The Best Decorated Homes*, and I didn't want to interrupt if she was on set." She paused as she pondered something. "Does Steven know I'm with you?"

"No." He shrugged. "Haven't spoken to him in a few days. He's in Washington. Congress is in session."

He stroked his goatee and tilted his head as a wide grin stretched from corner to corner of his mouth. The profiler in her knew where this conversation was going.

He leaned across the table. "Why didn't you tell your other half that you're safe with me?"

Sydney leaned in toward him, her head just inches away from his. "You mean why didn't I tell her that you're safe with *me*?"

He threw his head back in laughter, but then his facial expression turned serious. "Baby girl, I know you're Agent Chase and you know how to handle the bad guys but when you're with me, I'm the man."

She muffled a gulp, and her next breath lodged in her throat. She crossed her legs tightly to stifle the warm sensation that pulsed whenever he said something remotely sexual. But a passionate rush slammed through her body, and her right leg began to quiver. She stood and grabbed her purse.

"For your information, I'm grown. I don't tell my twin everything." So what if that was a lie? She wasn't ready to discuss Bryce with Megan because she wasn't sure what she'd say. Sydney needed to first figure out what the heck was wrong with her. "I'm going to the ladies' room."

She turned away from him and started down the sidewalk.

"You know, you're not the only one who understands body language. You forget I'm an attorney," he called after her as she groaned. As she continued her trek to the ladies' room, she heard his wicked laugh in the background.

Once there, she splashed water on her face, hoping to cool down her body. This was ridiculous. Sydney couldn't believe she actually found herself lusting after the one man she never thought in a million years she would ever want. He was cocky and arrogant even though he probably just thought he was confident and sure of himself, which he was. And that turned her on even more, especially his serious expression when his jaw was clenched and his eyes turned dark as coal. He was in full control, and she craved to have him in control over her mind and body just as he had when he had bestowed that kiss upon her. That stupid kiss that started all her crazy thinking that she could actually fall for him. Not going to happen.

She exhaled and splashed water on her face once more, and then headed back toward the picnic bench. Sydney slid her shades over her eyes as his eyes caught hers in a knowing stare. He stood by the passenger side of the SUV and tossed her the keys, which she caught.

"You drive."

They rode in silence for a while as Bryce checked and returned emails on his cell phone. She was glad for the quiet between them and preferred listening to the Tony! Toni! Toné! CD he'd popped in when they started back on the road.

He placed his phone in the console between them and cleared his throat. "So...I was thinking we can stop over and rest in Saint Louis tonight and start fresh in the morning unless you wanted to stop in Memphis and see your cousins."

"No, Saint Louis is fine."

While her original plan had been to stop in Memphis and say hello to her cousins Bria and Raven Arrington, that she was now traveling with Bryce made her change her mind. She still hadn't come to grips with the fact that she had begun to see him in a different light and actually thought she was attracted to him. Considering no one in her immediate family or Bryce's family knew they were traveling together, she'd rather keep it that way before Megan—the hopeless romantic—started making wedding plans.

He cleared his throat and turned toward her. "Before I knew you were tagging along, I'd reserved a suite at the Ritz-Carlton. They just sent me a confirmation email—"

"I can't afford the Ritz," she answered abruptly, shooting him a glance.

"Syd, I got this. Okay? It's a very large suite with two bathrooms and a separate bedroom. There's a pull-out sofa in the living room. I'll sleep there."

She exhaled even though he'd still be close by. "Well…thank you, and I'll fill the tank up the next time we stop…" She glanced at the gas gauge. "Which may be soon."

"No, you don't have to do that. I invited you to come with me. Besides, your car is in the shop. Save your money."

There he goes being nice again.

"Bryce…"

"Don't worry about it. Just enjoy your vacation. You deserve it," he said sincerely, grabbing his cell phone as it rang.

For the next hour or so he talked on the phone about his law firm with his accountant, and Sydney was glad his focus was off her as he discussed numbers, employees and clients. She said a little prayer that she could get through the next week without doing something she knew she *wouldn't* regret.

Chapter 5

Sydney lounged on the bed in the luxurious suite at the Ritz-Carlton. They'd arrived around nine and had eaten dinner in the hotel restaurant. She was drained from their long trip and was thankful that Bryce had run into a gentleman who was a friend of his father's. The two men had talked during most of their dinner about politics and world events. She'd excused herself when the dessert arrived—taking hers to go—and retreated upstairs to take a long shower in the beautiful marbled bathroom. Luckily, there were two bathrooms and the other one was connected to the parlor, where Bryce would sleep.

She'd received another text message from Megan during dinner but waited until she was alone to respond. Sydney sent a simple text back telling her sister that she was in Saint Louis for the night and was going to bed. As soon as she sent it, Megan called. Sydney reluctantly answered the phone and hoped their conversation would be brief.

"Hey, sissy," Sydney said, pressing the mute button on the flat-screen television.

"Hey. Just wanted to make sure you weren't still driving. So you're in Saint Louis? I thought you were going to stop over in Memphis."

"I was, but I went ahead and drove the extra hour." She hated lying to her sister. "But I did inform Aunt Darla that I wasn't coming."

"Oh…okay. I just spoke to Steven, and he said Bryce was spending the night at the Ritz in Saint Louis. How ironic is that? You're both in the same city. I guess it's a good stopping point."

"Hopefully I won't run into the jerk." She hoped she sounded convincing enough and prayed he didn't walk in and say anything. After hopping off the bed, she escaped to the bathroom, closed the door and sat on the edge of the oversize bathtub.

"Where are you staying?"

In a place better than my house.

"Um…at some Marriott," she said, thinking it wasn't a total lie. The Ritz was owned by Marriott. "You know I belong to their rewards program. Gotta get those points." She let out a fake yawn, which ended up turning into a real one followed by one from Megan, as well.

"Going to let you go. I have a big day tomorrow on set. They're installing the kitchen appliances, and

I have a feeling the refrigerator may not fit in the provided space."

"I'm sure it'll work out."

"Let's hope so. Send me a text before you leave in the morning. I'll be up at six for hair and makeup, but I'll call you when I can."

After hanging up and turning off her cell phone, Sydney lay back on the bed and continued to flip through the channels watching nothing in particular. A knock sounded at the bedroom door. She sat all the way up. She was hoping she wouldn't have to see Bryce until the morning. They'd agreed to eat breakfast at seven in the hotel's restaurant and hit the road after that.

"Come in."

"Hey. I'm back from dinner." Bryce strolled into the room and sat in one of the wingback chairs by the window. She noticed his eyes divert their attention briefly to the clothes she had set out for tomorrow on the chair opposite his. A glimmer twinkled in his eyes when he noticed her black lace bra and panties flung on top.

"What can I do for you?"

His gaze landed on her face, the glimmer still present. "First of all, never ask a man who finds you extremely attractive what you can do for him. Especially when you're propped up in the bed wearing a tank top and boy shorts."

She'd completely forgotten what she was wearing. She pulled the plush down comforter up to her chin. "Whatever." She tried to shrug it off but her defenses around him were becoming lower and lower with every conversation.

"You wanna go for a motorcycle ride with me?"

She glanced at the clock on the nightstand. "It's after eleven o'clock."

"That's the perfect time to go."

"It's freezing outside," she stated matter-of-factly. "And we're in a strange city."

He stood and grabbed her bra from the chair, tossing it to her. "Change clothes and grab your helmet. We'll take my bike."

"I'll only go if you let me drive."

"Not a problem," he said with the most sinful smile she'd ever seen on a man.

Twenty minutes later, they were in the parking garage as Sydney watched Bryce back his Harley off the trailer.

"I'll take it out through the parking garage, and we'll switch when we get out front." He slid his helmet on his head and drove around to her side. "You know the passenger rules, right?"

"Lean with you, don't make any hand signals, don't put my feet on the ground and pay attention to traffic just in case you have to brake or speed up unexpectedly. Oh, and don't knock helmets. I hate that."

"And the most important one is…" He paused, his eyes roaming over her figure. "Keep looking hella sexy in those leather pants." His lazy gaze lingered on her hips as he ran his tongue over his bottom lip. "Damn, you're fine, woman."

She couldn't help but smile. "Thank you. You don't look half-bad yourself in your jeans and leather jacket."

An astonished expression progressed over his face. "A seductive smile and a compliment from Agent Chase? I should've kissed those succulent lips a long time ago," he stated in a dangerous tone.

Goose bumps ran rampant over her skin and that darn twinge was back between her thighs. "Wouldn't have worked," she said, trying not to break her composure. "You caught me off guard in the hospital. I wasn't feeling my best because if I was, I would've drop-kicked you." She winked and placed her helmet on and took a step toward the bike, but he zoomed a few feet away from her.

"Stop playing with me," she shouted. "You know I can chase after you."

He backed up to her and lifted the visor, flashing a mischievous smile. "Really? You'd chase after me? I'll keep that in mind. Come on. Let's go."

She hesitated, then threw her leg over the seat and hopped up behind him, placing her hands on his shoulders.

He gazed at her over his shoulder. "Hold on around my waist."

She glided her hands down and secured them around his waist as her breasts mashed into his back. She backed up a little bit, but he yelled out. "Doesn't bother me."

He shot off, and the immediate exhilaration that she loved transpired. While it was a short distance, he exuded a power she hadn't experienced with him and became disappointed when he stopped and got off. She sort of wished she hadn't volunteered to drive. Holding on to him made her feel safe and secure. That was rare when she was with a man. She was more than capable of defending herself. But spending time with Bryce lately made her feel protected by him. She wasn't quite sure what to do with that newfound realization. The more time she spent with him, the more she wanted to learn about what made him tick. What made him the man that he was; the man she hadn't given herself the opportunity to get to know until now because she was always too busy arguing with him.

She slid her body up the seat and adjusted the mirrors. Lifting the visor of his helmet, he approached the front of the bike.

"Have you ever had anyone behind you before?" he asked with a raised eyebrow.

"Will you stop with all the sexual innuendos and let's go."

"Oh, no. I'm serious. This is my favorite motorcycle, and I don't let just anyone drive it. In fact, you're the first person, so just be careful."

She kicked up the kickstand and revved the engine. "Get on or I'm leaving without you."

Bryce rubbed the bike's left handle and climbed onto the back, scooting all the way up to her bottom. He sensually wrapped his hands around her waist, resting his hands on her pelvis. His chest was like a brick wall slammed against her back and his strong, long legs pressed against hers.

How on earth did I form my mouth to say I wanted to drive? I can't concentrate and I haven't even started.

"Are you comfortable back there?" she asked. Even though he drove a motorcycle, she knew that some drivers didn't necessarily like to be passengers. However, she doubted that was the case with him. He was more concerned about his precious bike.

"Very. You ever drove anything this big?"

"My motorcycle is about this size."

He chuckled, and she turned around to look at him, but his visor was down. She wasn't sure if he was serious or spewing more innuendos.

She yelled out, "I can handle it."

He made the go signal over her shoulder and slapped the side of her hip.

"We'll see," he called out.

She started off slow to get used to the motorcycle. It may not have been much bigger than hers, but it was a different engine. It purred under her, and she instantly fell in love with it. She was relaxed as the cold air blew around them yet warm and secure in his arms. The sensation of raw pleasure raced through her as his embrace held her close against his chest. When she turned the corner, he leaned with her perfectly and completely in sync. He was definitely a skilled rider and driver. She rarely had passengers because most people didn't feel comfortable and couldn't remember all the simple yet important rules. However, Bryce seemed to know which way she was going to turn or how fast she was going to go before she even did so. He was the ideal rider.

When she turned onto the interstate, his right hand glided down her thigh and back up under her leather jacket until he reached the button on her pants and popped it open. His finger teased along her panty line, and she sped up. She leaned back into him, wanting to close her eyes to enjoy him. She pulled off at the next exit and was caught at the red light.

"Are you comfortable?" he shouted, stopping the perusal of her panty line for a moment.

"Yes," she yelled back. She shifted in the seat until she could feel an erection through his pants.

He slid his hand farther into her panties, massaging the entire mound with his hand. He kneaded her slowly yet deeply, causing heavy waves to crash inside her. It was so much more than the sensations she'd experienced when he'd kissed her. She reached her hand back, wanting to feel his face, but remembered he was wearing a helmet. With his free hand, he lifted his visor and took her gloved hand in his, kissing the palm before placing a finger in between his lips. The warmth of his mouth seeped through to her skin and she let out a moan so loud she was sure it could be heard through her helmet. She removed her hand once the light changed to green, and he settled his arm back around her waist, holding her nestled against him.

Sydney veered left in order to zoom across the bridge to turn onto the interstate and landed at another red light in the turning lane. She didn't want to go too far from the hotel in an unfamiliar city. Plus, Bryce's hand in her panties caused her to lose what little concentration she had left. While she enjoyed their adventure, safety was key. She removed his hand and placed it back on her waist just as the light changed.

They made it back to the hotel moments later. She'd driven so fast she was surprised a cop didn't pull her over, but the ride had revved her up more than the engine of the motorcycle. She parked in the empty space next to his SUV and hopped off immediately. She skirted away from him to the other side of the Range Rover, where she zipped up her pants and fastened the button.

"Syd?"

She took off her helmet. "What?" She was flustered, and she hated appearing that way in front of him,

"You all right?" he asked with concern, turning her around to face him. "You didn't enjoy our ride?"

"Yes…and no. I lost all concentration when you were roaming your hands everywhere. While I'm not saying I didn't enjoy it, that wasn't very safe." Even though she felt completely safe in his arms.

He pulled her into his embrace and pushed them into a corner that was hidden by his SUV. "We're not on the motorcycle now."

Bryce's lips closed over hers, kissing her ferociously and deeply, not holding back. And she didn't want him to. She'd longed to feel his lips and tongue again and reached up to his face, pulling him deeper into her mouth. Their moans filled the cold air, and she couldn't distinguish hers from his. His hands left her body for a moment as he took his gloves off and tossed them on the ground. He ran his warm palms under her jacket and down to her bottom. Squeezing it hard, he brought it toward him, pressing her body tight against his.

His hands and lips on her were pure torture. Every piece of her was spiked with sheer stimulation just from his touch, no matter how slight it was. Her body shook with excitement as he lifted her, and she wrapped her legs around his waist, holding on to his manly shoulders tightly. But not from the fear of being dropped, but because orgasmic sensations had begun to wreak havoc through her, and she didn't know how much she could handle despite the fact she'd just told him she could. However, she hadn't expected so much wild, crazy passion from him. He was in total control over her, and she loved every minute of the hot journey he was steering them on.

His warm tongue traveled down her neck, sucking and taunting. Her moans became louder and echoed in the parking garage, but she didn't care who heard or saw as long as he continued to ravish her senseless.

Pulling his lips from hers—his glazed eyes full of vigor—he stared her down as if he were going to tear her to pieces that very moment. Her chest heaved up and down as he set her back on the ground and ran his hands through her hair, pulling her lips to his, but he didn't kiss her.

"You wanna finish this upstairs?" he whispered on

her mouth. "We can make love all over the suite. All night..."

Fear and panic rose in her, and she shoved him back toward his Range Rover. His eyes turned into confused saucers as he held his gaze firm with hers. "Syd, what's wrong?"

"Make love? I don't even like you!" she shouted, storming away from him, but he followed, pulling her back against his chest and holding her hands gently by the wrists.

"And yet your kisses and erotic moans tell a completely different story," he calmly stated.

She yanked away and picked up her helmet from the ground, sitting it on the motorcycle as she tried to make sense of what was happening to her. He was driving her insane with passion and lust. She didn't know what to make of it.

He stepped toward her with the bike in between them. "What are you so scared of? Obviously there's something between us."

She shook her head. "The only things we have in common are motorcycles and that our siblings are married. That's it."

Sydney turned on her heel and walked in a fast pace toward the elevator. Groaning, she pushed the button rapidly. The doors opened and she stepped inside, grateful for the escape from him.

Once she was settled back in the suite, Sydney locked the bedroom door, tossed off her clothes and dived under the comforter. She hoped he wouldn't try to finish their conversation when he returned from securing his motorcycle. She hated to admit she had enjoyed the ride and their second kiss. His scent was once again embedded in her skin and it was even stronger now that she was under the comforter. She yanked it off and sat up as the suite door opened and closed. His footsteps sounded and stopped as she caught her breath. She sensed him outside of the bedroom door, but then she heard his bathroom door shut and the water from the shower.

Exhaling, she lay back onto the bed. If she wasn't stuck with her huge suitcase and it weren't winter, she'd have jumped on her beloved Harley, Pretty in Pink, and jetted away. Since none of that was possible, she decided that tomorrow she would put on her game face and not let Bryce get the best of her.

Chapter 6

They'd been on the road for an hour in complete silence except when Bryce had asked Sydney what kind of music she wanted to listen to. She'd shrugged and barely whispered, "Doesn't matter" before continuing to flip through the pages in her magazine so hard that one actually ripped. He had to muffle a chuckle as she huffed and instead placed his focus on the long road ahead. Both the actual highway and the one with her.

He honestly hadn't known what to expect that morning. A part of him was surprised she hadn't hightailed it out of there in the middle of the night on her motorcycle. When she'd tiptoed out of her room at five in the morning, that was what he'd thought she was doing but instead, she'd pulled a bottle of water from the cooler and ducked back into her room.

He couldn't figure out what had gone wrong. They were having a great time. The flirting and the motorcycle ride had all led up to their rendezvous on the wall. Heck, she was a hot sex kitten practically devouring him, but something made her think twice, and she'd stopped the passion that had erupted between them. He wasn't necessarily upset about that. More than anything, he wanted to know what had caused her to push him away physically and emotionally. The truth was he was enjoying spending time with her and getting to know a different side of her.

"Syd?" he asked uneasily.

Closing the magazine, she inhaled but didn't look his way. "Yes?" Her voice was calm but had a hint of agitation.

"I just want to apologize if I upset you last night. I didn't mean to. I thought we were having a great time on the trip and on the motorcycle. You know, just getting to know each other better in general."

She exhaled and looked at him for the first time since last night. "I think that being in close quarters with you, especially on the motorcycle, may have caused us to want to continue that blissful high you have when you're riding. Personally, I don't think there's anything between us… It was the sexiness of the ride. You just happened to be there during the invigorating thrill I get when on a motorcycle."

"Mmm…yeah." Bryce nodded, then paused. "I suppose you're right. Here I was on the back of my own motorcycle with a gorgeous woman, holding you close to me and listening to the stimulating moans you let out because you were driving my favorite bike. So…sure, it was the sexiness of the ride that caused us to want more of each other."

"Yep. I totally agree."

Bryce didn't know if he believed any of what he said. True, the midnight ride had stimulated some kind of passion and desire; however, they weren't new feelings. He'd just never thought he'd have an opportunity to demonstrate them. After the kiss in the hospital, kissing her again was all he'd thought about. Last night, he'd been given another chance and he'd run with it. He just hoped the occasion arose once more but he knew how Syd thought. He knew she would make sure to never ride on the same motorcycle ever again.

Syd pretended to read an article on the latest fashion trends. She had no interest in it, but anything to avoid talking to him, even though as the copilot she did make sure the music stayed upbeat. She was glad they were somewhat on the same page when it came to what happened last night. She'd had male passengers every blue moon, and none of them had turned her on like Bryce had. Then again, none of them had dared to slide a hand into her panties, for if they'd done so, she would've pulled over and left them on the side of the road.

Bryce had stimulated more than just the spot that made her a woman. He'd also stimulated her thought process. She was seeing him in a different light with each passing moment they spent together. His discussions on growing up as a Monroe and how family-oriented he was were totally unexpected. The fact that he'd wanted to work at a law firm first instead of opening his own impressed her. He was a Monroe, after all. He could've easily started a firm straight out of law school, but the fact that he didn't spoke volumes. It made her think about her present job situation.

For once in her life she didn't miss it. Usually while on vacation, she'd still think about a case and would call Mumford if she had a hunch about something. However, this time she hadn't even thought about work and when she saw the voice mail from Watkins, she didn't call him back right away.

"So when do you think your firm will be up and running?" she asked after a while. The magazine no longer held her interest, and he kept changing his satellite radio stations and mumbling about nothing being on the radio worth listening to.

"I close on the building in a few weeks. It's located in the midtown area of Peachtree not far from Atlantic Station. It's two stories and has plenty of space for the law library, conference rooms and offices for at least twenty lawyers along with paralegals and legal secretaries."

"Oh, you intend to have that many?"

"Not at first. I have a few friends who are interested, and I have some people on my list that I'd like to persuade to work with me. I want a variety, and not just criminal law. Even though that will be the main focus for my cases, of course. But I'm looking into child advocacy lawyers, as well. The children in the foster care and adoption agencies need a voice. Some of the children I tutor at the Monroe Community Center are in the system, and it breaks my heart that their needs aren't being met by the system or by the so-called foster parents who only want to collect a check. Explain to me why foster parents are picking up their children in Mercedes and Escalades, carrying expensive purses and wearing designer duds. Yet the poor kid walks out to the car with raggedy shoes and jeans that are too small? And I know it's not all foster parents, but the ones who do are giving the ones who provide love and stability a bad reputation, as well."

"I didn't realize you tutored at the center." *Or had an interest in the well-being of foster children.*

"Yep, usually on the weekends. I went there after I left your house on Saturday morning for a few hours. The students are preparing for the Georgia Milestone Assessment Test. That's why I left so early. The workshop is from eight to noon every Saturday until testing. Of course, I'm missing this Saturday, but your cousin Tiffani is going to take my group along with hers."

"Oh…I didn't realize she was tutoring there." Sydney hadn't spoken to Tiffani in a few weeks or really anyone since the GBI had begun working on two big cases. She hated missing out on things. She'd barely made it to Megan and Steven's one-year anniversary celebration earlier that year.

"She just started a few weeks ago. Megan suggested her to me considering Tiffani is a third-grade teacher and needed some extra money. She brings KJ along. That kid is something else. Such a bright young man."

"Yep, he's a sweetheart. I'm just glad that Tiffani is finally moving on with her life as best as possible since her husband's death three years ago. I'm sure raising Keith Jr. has to be overwhelming, but she never complains. Aunt Betty and Uncle John spoil their grandson rotten."

"Yep. He has a good family foundation, which is important. It truly takes a village to raise a child."

Sydney was somewhat still in shock that he tutored. Not that she didn't think he could. Bryce was highly intelligent, but she didn't know where he found the time. She didn't think his schedule permitted it, or his personality. Plus, the community center had always been Steven's project. But since he spent a lot of time in Washington, DC, when Congress was in session, he wasn't able to commit as often as he used to.

"So what do you tutor?"

"English and math for the Georgia Milestone workshop, but during the school year, homework or other projects. During the summer, I work with kindergarteners going into first grade who need assistance with their sight words and putting them together in order to read and write sentences."

She tilted her head with a wrinkled brow. "Are you an attorney or a teacher?"

He laughed, but then his face turned serious. "Just a concerned person who believes in education. I had a good life growing up. I never had to worry about where my next meal was coming from, would I have clean clothes to wear or whether or not I had enough money for college. The children at the community center don't have the same advantages, which was one of the reasons why Steven and I opened it."

"I didn't know you had anything to do with it. I remember when it opened years ago, there was a segment on the news, but your father and Steven were the only ones giving the tour and being interviewed. I don't remember you being there."

"I was there, but it was election year for both of them. I'm not a politician. No need for me to be on camera. They needed votes. Not why we opened it, but good press for the Monroe family. Besides, I prefer to stay in the background. I don't care about accolades, I just want a safe and nurturing environment for the children to go after school."

He rubbed his goatee, which meant he was pondering something. He glanced at her and then sped up to pass a truck, using on his left-hand side. Once he slowed down and moved back to the right, he smirked and tapped her knee.

"So, if I remember correctly, the following week after the news segment I saw you at the courthouse, and you glared at me when you walked by as I was stepping off the elevator. You mumbled something like '*I guess you had better things to do*' in your sassy, disapproving tone. I couldn't figure out what the hell you were talking about, but now I know. You thought I wasn't involved. You thought I was an arrogant ass who didn't have time for such things. Am I right?"

She closed her eyes and took a breath in. Yep, he was right. That was exactly what she'd thought for almost five years. Now she wasn't so sure. Normally, she could figure people out within the first few minutes of meeting them. That was her job. But Bryce had always remained a mystery to her until now.

Placing her legs underneath her in the oversized seat, she slid her shades up onto her head and turned her body toward him.

"That's exactly what I thought, but I'm beginning to see you in a whole different light, and I have to admit I'm impressed," she said, lowering her eyes and running her fingers through her hair. "You're concerned about your family and the welfare of the children you service at the center. Apparently, you may have more to do with its conception than Steven. You're a good guy, after all. I was wrong."

He grabbed her hand, and a pleased curl of a smile formed. "I'm glad you're beginning to see me for who I am. I think one of the reasons why you and others think I'm some arrogant, conceited rich guy is because of how I am in court. I can't show weakness. I can't back down. I refuse to lose a case, and if I do, it damn sure wasn't because I didn't give it my all to prove my client's innocence."

"That makes total sense even though you still have an air of confidence and authority," she said, not believing they were having a heart-to-heart conversation. "You exude that regardless."

He squeezed her hand before letting it go to place both hands on the steering wheel to pass another eighteen-wheeler truck. She sort of liked him holding her hand and hoped he'd hurry up and pass the truck.

"And the same with you. In your position, you have to be a tough woman, especially when you're probably the only one in a room full of agents and hardened criminals. You can't show weakness. No time to be the *girlie girl*. Your twin inherited that from your mother. You, on the other hand, you have that no-nonsense, take-no-prisoners attitude from your dad. Luckily, I've seen the tender side of you."

"Well, I guess we've both learned a lot about each other during this trip." Her thoughts took her back to last night on the motorcycle. She'd also learned that his hand could give her a mind-blowing orgasm and his tongue was lethal and should be arrested for the passionate assault on her lips and neck. Also, he could hold her up for a long period of time without weakening his arms around her or stopping for a breath while they kissed. Too bad she wouldn't experience that again. She squirmed in her seat and placed her shades over her eyes once more.

"I've also learned that you hide behind your shades. It's a cloudy day, Syd."

Blood rushed into her cheeks at Bryce's realization. She tossed the shades into the console between them and looked his way.

He ran a finger along her cheek that evoked prickly tingles over her at his subtle, warm touch. "Yep. There's the fire I know. Stop hiding it. It's one of my favorite things about you."

"I like to protect my eyes from the sun. That's all."

"Um…the sun is hiding behind the clouds…" He laughed, patting her on the knee. He gave it a quick squeeze, then tenderly slid his hand off her and back on the steering wheel. She noted the tight way he held it and the scrunch of his brow. A stiffness was forming again, and the last thing she wanted was more sexual tension with him. She offered to drive, and they switched a few moments later. That way she'd have to concentrate on the road and not the fact that she wanted him.

"I need to confess something to you," Syd started as she turned onto the interstate.

It was later in the evening. They'd stopped for dinner and decided to continue on for another four hours before resting for the night and driving the last six hours in the morning.

Bryce turned the radio down and placed his focus on her. He was hoping she would say she wanted to explore them getting to know each other on a more intimate level. That was definitely a road he wanted to take with her.

"I'm not happy with my career anymore."

Okay, so he wasn't expecting that detour; however,

he blocked his thoughts of seducing her considering the information she'd just revealed was serious.

"I'm surprised to hear that. I thought you loved being a criminal profiler."

"I do, but I don't like the long hours anymore. I don't like not seeing my home for two days because I've spent the night at headquarters. I don't like passing out at work and waking up in the hospital. That wasn't the first time. My health and well-being are important. My family is worried about me, especially my sister. We have twin senses, so when something is wrong with me, she feels it and vice versa. I'm not saying I'm going to quit tomorrow, but I do need to begin looking at other options."

"And have you?"

"Well, I do have my law degree from University of Georgia, but I haven't taken the bar exam. It's ironic when you mentioned hiring a child advocacy attorney because that's the direction I'd thought about heading in when I was in law school."

"Take the bar and come work for me."

"I don't think you and I working together would be a great idea," she said, shaking her head. "We'd butt heads."

Plus, he wouldn't get any work done with her around. He would be too busy calculating ways to seduce her in his office, her office and the conference room. "Maybe you're right. However, I think you should go ahead and take the bar."

"I've been studying on and off for it for a few years.

Mostly off because I haven't had the time. It's just an idea that's been in my head for a while. I believe this is the first time I've actually said it out loud." A look of relief crossed over her face as she exhaled.

"You haven't told your family?"

"No. Of course, my parents are always suggesting I leave the GBI. Braxton says whatever makes me happy, and Megan, the worrywart when it comes to me, of course wants me to go into another field."

"I'm glad you felt you could confide in me," he said sincerely.

"Well, you're sort of in the same boat. Everyone else I know isn't making drastic changes in their careers. Plus, when you said, 'There comes a time when you have to move on. When you've outgrown where you are,' that struck something in me. I think passing out at work was a wake-up call. Now I just need to figure out my next move."

"Well, your boss gave you a month off. Use this time to do some soul-searching. Maybe even join a study group for the bar and then take it. At least you'd have it just in case you decide being a criminal profiler just isn't for you anymore. However, you're an amazing profiler and investigator, so you'd be missed in the field."

"Hmm…a lot to think about, but in the meantime, I'm ready to get to Vegas and have fun."

"I hear you. You want me to drive?"

"Nope, I'm good. Can't wait to get to the hotel, though. I'm ready to take a shower and climb into bed."

"Me, too."

Too bad it wouldn't be with her. After last night's escapade, they reserved separate rooms for the night. That didn't mean he was going to give up on pursuing her. They'd made progress that day, which was a step in the direction he was steering them.

Chapter 7

"Syd. Wake up."

Sydney peeked out from the slits of her eyes at the blaring afternoon sun. "Close the blinds, please," she mumbled, sliding her shades down from the top of her head.

They'd left around nine in the morning after grabbing breakfast. Bryce offered to drive the last hours to Las Vegas, and she didn't complain. Instead, she watched movies in the backseat until her eyelids became heavy and she'd laid down on the comfortable leather.

"There are no blinds to close. We're on the Vegas Strip, babe."

She sat all the way up and leaned over the console to peer out the huge windshield of his Range Rover. She'd never been to Vegas before and was in awe over the casinos and hotels flanking both sides of the street. She couldn't wait to see it lit up at night in all its magical glory. However, for now she was excited when he turned in to the Bellagio and she saw groups of motorcyclists standing around in biker gear and on their bikes heading out into the Strip. In one swoop, she slid back over to the front and plopped into the passenger seat.

"Next time, give me a warning. I thought you were about to straddle me." He glanced at her with a delicious smile and winked. "Not that I would've minded."

Sydney reached to the backseat and grabbed her black leather peplum jacket and placed it on over her white fitted T-shirt.

"In your sweet dreams, Counselor."

"You've been there, too," Bryce mumbled under his breath.

"Whatever."

They must have been on the same wavelength, because last night he'd shown up in her dreams, as well. However, they were only daydreams as she stayed up half the night reliving their motorcycle ride and what happened afterward. She couldn't jar her thoughts from it. Being held in his muscular embrace was pure heaven. His strong arms encircling her while he seductively weaved his fingers in her hair, causing her blood to boil. The passion that had been stirred that night was new and wild. She'd never felt so alive and sexual before with a man. She craved to experience what he could teach her. Just by the way his lips devoured her and how his hands traveled over her body, she knew she'd be in for an exhilarating treat. He was all man. She'd never felt like a natural woman until the other night when he'd awakened a lust and desire so strong that she needed to witness for herself every single erotic pleasure she knew he could offer. She just hoped she could handle him.

Out of all the men in the world, why did it have to be him?

"I think I'll just have my SUV valet-parked, and we can self-park the bikes. I don't see needing my Rover for the rest of the trip. Do you?"

His deep voice pulled her out of her amorous thoughts. For a moment, she was back against the wall with a man she wasn't sure she could resist for much longer.

"No. I think that's a great idea," she croaked out.

Bryce dropped her off at the front, and a bellhop grabbed all of their belongings while he saw to the parking of the vehicles. She fished around in her purse for her wallet as she stood in a long line to check in. It was around three o'clock, so she really hoped her room was ready.

"Hey." She looked to her left to see Bryce towering over her. "I got the motorcycles in the self-parking lot with tons of other motorcycles, including a few other pink ones."

"Nothing is wrong with a pink bike."

"You'll never catch me on it except to take it off my trailer." He cleared his throat. "So I guess after we check into our room…rooms, we can pick up our registration information."

"That's cool. I registered for some events for tomorrow. I think I may rest for a while and then go down to the meet-and-greet social tonight. I think it starts at six. What are you doing?"

"Um…well I was going to go to the meet and greet."

"Okay, I'll meet you in the lobby around five forty-five." Realizing she was next, she pulled her wallet out. "Hello, I'm Sydney Chase," she said to a young lady with a pleasant smile.

"Good afternoon, Ms. Chase. I'm Debbie. Just give me a moment to find your name in the system," Debbie said, typing quickly along the keys with a frown. "Mmm… are you here for the bike fest?" she asked as her eyes scanned over Syd's leather jacket.

"Yes."

"When did you make your reservation?" Debbie typed quickly again and frowned.

"On Monday. Maybe you're spelling my name wrong. It's *S-Y-D-N-E-Y*. My mom wanted to be different," Sydney joked with a smile as she tried not to worry. It had been a last-minute reservation, but there had been a few rooms left.

"I'll try that way."

However, the frown appeared again, and Bryce stepped in.

"Is there a problem, Debbie?" he asked in his lawyer voice that Sydney knew quite well, having been cross-examined by it on the stand.

"Well, it says the reservation has been canceled."

Syd banged her hand on the counter. "What? I never

canceled. There must be some mistake," she said in a curt tone.

Bryce rubbed her back. "Calm down, Syd. I'm sure they have another room available."

"No, actually, everything is booked because of the motorcycle fest and about five other conferences and events."

Sydney's heart sank. She'd come came all this way and now didn't have a place to crash. There were some other hotels in walking distance, but she really wanted to stay at the Bellagio.

"You can stay with me," Bryce suggested with a wink as if he heard her thoughts. "Let's look up mine. Bryce Monroe. I made my reservation a few months back."

Once again, Debbie's fingers moved rapidly, and her smile reappeared. "Yes, Mr. Monroe. You have a Salone Suite. Do you need one or two keys?"

Bryce stared down at Sydney with a raised wicked eyebrow and a sly smile. Her breathing halted and tingles of sweat formed on her hairline. The last time that had happened, she'd passed out.

"Do I need two keys, Syd?" he asked in a heavy, deep tone, causing her heart to skip a beat or three and then pound uncontrollably against her chest.

She turned toward Debbie because if she looked at him a millisecond longer, she'd have jumped him right there in the middle of the lobby in front of at least one hundred people. "You said it was a suite?"

"Yes, Ms. Chase. A very nice suite."

She thought about their sleeping arrangement last time. Knowing Bryce, it was one of the oversize suites with the separate bedroom that she'd glanced at on the website when making her reservation; they were well out of her budget. "Okay…two keys, and put half of it on my card," she said with a slight gulp, handing Debbie the card, but Bryce snatched it away and slid it into his front pocket.

"Nonsense. I got this." He handed Debbie his black card, which she immediately swiped and handed back.

"Bryce!"

"Babe, let's just check in. You can give me your sassy lip later, but there are people in line behind us."

Twenty minutes later, they were in the suite as Sydney stood in front of him tapping her foot as he tried his best to look confused. She was waiting impatiently for the bellhop to place their luggage in the room and for Bryce to give him a tip. Once the young bellhop left with a wide smile at the generous one-hundred-dollar bill, Sydney turned around with her arms out like a bird ready for takeoff. She faced him again, stepping into his personal space.

"This is not a suite," she said through clenched teeth.

He smiled mischievously. "Yes, it is. Just because it doesn't have a separate living room and a true bedroom with a door doesn't mean it's not a suite. This is not an average hotel, grasshopper. This is a corner suite with a view of the fountains. And it does have a separate living area. We're standing in it. The bed is way over there." He pointed to a bed that was on the opposite side of the room, facing one of the corner windows. "The sofa is a bed, as well, like last time."

"In the same room."

"An eight-hundred-square-foot room." He glanced around it before settling his eyes back on hers. "It's the size of my apartment in college." He shrugged with a naughty grin as his eyes twinkled.

"You're finding all of this funny, aren't you?"

"I just love seeing you angry. I find it irresistibly sexy," he answered in a tantalizing way that caused passionate waves of heat to ripple through her body and end at the one place she longed for him to be.

She walked away from him to peer out the window at the beautiful Bellagio fountains and to stop herself from attacking him. If she had to be in the same room, at least she'd have a spectacular view. While the water shooting up was lovely, she was frustrated. Sexually, that is. How could she contain herself and her feelings if he was in the same room for the next three nights without wanting to rip him apart? Well, mainly his shirt. So she could get to his powerful, strapping chest in order to run her hand down its hardness and end up at the top of his belt. The belt that she wanted to yank out of the loops and toss across the room, then unzip his pants so she could see and feel in person his throbbing erection that had rubbed in between her legs. She had craved seeing it that night but unfortunately fear had set in, which was rare for her, and she'd had to push him away. She had to get away from him so she could think clearly.

However, all she could think about was being seduced by him and enjoying every minute of the ride.

The ringing of Bryce's cell phone startled her out of her wild escapade. He sat on the couch in the sitting area and propped his feet on the table.

"Hello? Oh, hi, Mrs. Thomas. How are you?" Bryce asked in a professional yet kindhearted tone.

Sydney glanced at him over her shoulder to see a strained and concerned expression as he nodded his head.

"Oh…that's not good. That's not good at all."

Placing his head on his forehead, he continued listening, rising out of his seat and striding toward the window.

"I'm out of town at the moment. However, I have my laptop so I can get started on this right away for you." He glanced around the room and motioned to Sydney as if he were writing on his hand. Realizing he needed pen and paper, she spotted a hotel pen and notepad on the desk and handed them to him. He mouthed "thank you" to her while listening to Mrs. Thomas and jotted down the information.

"Okay, I promise you I'll take care of this…What?… You're kidding, right? When have I ever sent you a bill in the past nine years?" He laughed and sat back on the couch. "Yes, your peach cobbler is the bomb! That will be perfect. When is your niece coming?…Okay, have her take you by the bank. I'm going to transfer some money into your account…No…no…It's not up for debate. I'll be back sometime on Tuesday night, but

I promise to come over first thing Wednesday morning, and you better still have heat. Take care of that today. I'll call your niece in a bit."

After he said goodbye, he tossed the phone onto the couch and washed his hands down his face. Sydney stared at him as he sat silently in contemplation mode. She'd seen it before, usually in court when he needed to change his strategy.

"What's wrong?" she asked.

"One of my clients is having a hard time."

"She was arrested for something?"

"Oh…no. Even though I'm a criminal attorney, I do take on noncriminal clients, usually someone who is being wronged, and always pro bono."

She had no idea he did things like that. He was always on the nightly news being interviewed for his criminal trials. She didn't realize he took on pro bono cases, as well. The more and more she was around him, the more she understood that she didn't know him on the inside. Didn't know his heart. How could a top profiler for the GBI not see all the good in this man?

"Tell me about Mrs. Thomas."

"Mrs. Thomas used to work on my dad's campaign team years ago. She's a sweet old lady with a sassy mouth…kinda like you. I was a young cat then. Fresh out of law school. Just passed the bar. Dad suggested I take on some pro bono cases to get my feet wet before working at a big-time law firm. It's not like I needed the money, and I wasn't ready to start my own. I spent the first year and half working with mostly senior citizens like Mrs. Thomas. Anyway, she was injured on the job and had to stop working and was placed on disability. I worked with her against her place of employment because they didn't want to give her the correct amount that was in her contract. Needless to say, we settled. Trust me, I'm the last person you want to face in court."

"So I've seen. You're nothing to play with." And she knew that firsthand in more ways than one.

"Thanks." He smiled. "Anyway, I've helped other senior citizens throughout the years even while working for the firm. I think that's one of the reasons they were never going to make me a senior partner. They'd suggested numerous times for me to stop taking the outside pro bono cases, but I never would. Sure, they paid my salary, but what I made in a year, my investments and trust funds were still earning more than that on the interest alone. I told them several times they could fire me, and I'd happily walk, but I was their best attorney and a Monroe."

"I bet they regret losing you."

"Yep. I've gotten a few phone calls this week about going back. Nope. Don't think so." He stood and strode his long legs quickly across the room and grabbed his laptop bag by the door where the bellhop had placed their items.

"So what's wrong with Mrs. Thomas now?"

"Well, her husband died about a year ago, and she's getting the run around about his Social Security benefits," he stated, placing his laptop on the desk and turning it on. "She's on a strict income and is having some problems paying her bills. Plus, she has a lot of prescriptions, which is another issue. She never had children, but she's very close to her niece, Nancy, who I need to call in a moment. Nancy has been trying to assist, but now I need to get involved and I'm upset because she should've told me earlier this was happening. They always think they're bothering me when they're not."

Sydney sat in the middle of the huge king-size bed, tucking her feet underneath her. She was in complete awe of the man before her.

"So that's why you're sending her money? To pay for her gas bill, if I'm not mistaken?"

He snapped his fingers. "Yes, thank you for the reminder," he said, typing rapidly across the keys of his laptop. "It's not coming from me necessarily. My family has a charity set up for this purpose to help elderly or disabled people with bills, medications and such. My mother is over it. The gas company that Mrs. Thomas uses has sent a final notice that it will be turned off today at five o' clock. It's going to be freezing in Atlanta tonight and those people have the audacity to turn off a sweet old lady's heat. It pisses me off."

He turned to look at Sydney and tilted his head to the side. "Why are you looking me like that?"

She smirked and wondered how the heck she was looking. Was it showing on her face that she wanted him even more now? "Like what? I'm just listening to you and…realizing I didn't know you…well…that I didn't know—"

"That I cared? That I'm actually *not* a spoiled rich

brat from a privileged background? No…wait, I am rich with a privileged background, but it doesn't define me. It doesn't define my concern for others. And you thought Steven was the only one."

"I…" She stopped. She didn't know what to say. Did he have her figured out, as well?

"Well, look at this. Sydney Michelle Chase is speechless." He looked around the suite, then back at her. "Have you seen my cell phone? I gotta video this."

"No cell phone videos, especially with me sitting on the bed."

He raised a cocky eyebrow and bit his bottom lip. "That's the perfect place. Just joking, sort of."

"I will throw your cell phone into that fountain down there," she teased.

"So…you know about the cloud, right? I could've sent it to my email account in a flash."

"Whatever. Anyway, back on topic." Because the video phone conversation was making her curious to see what he would do if she invited him to join her on the bed. Instead, she got up and walked toward her suitcase by the door so she could iron her blouse for the evening and take her eyes off him. "Personally, I think the fact that you're rich has defined you, but in a good way. Because you have the money, you're more philanthropic."

"Jot this down in that profiler brain of yours. 'Bryce is actually a nice guy. I was wrong.'"

"It's been dutifully noted," she said, rolling her suitcase toward the bed and placing it on the bench in front of it.

"Thank you." After shutting his laptop, he slid it

into his bag and swung it over his shoulder. "Well, after looking over the forms on the website, I actually need to go down to the business center to use the printer and the fax machine. I should be back by six for the meet and greet, but if not I'll catch up with you."

"I can wait for you." She couldn't believe she said that, but for some reason she was actually saddened that he was leaving the room for a few hours and may even miss the first part of the meet and greet.

"No. Don't do that. You came to have fun." He slid one of the key cards off the coffee table and slipped it in his pocket. "Text me if you need to," he said, shutting the door.

"Will do."

Bryce made it back upstairs after handling everything for Mrs. Thomas. He'd also scheduled a meeting the following week to speak with the Social Security office about her benefits. They were giving her the runaround, but with him on her side, she didn't have to worry.

A sweet orchid scent hit his nose as he entered the suite, and he knew it instantly. It was Syd's perfume. She hadn't used any on the road trip because she'd mentioned something about being enclosed in the SUV and didn't want to awaken her sinuses. Now she'd sprayed it on before heading down to the meet and greet that he'd finally convinced her over a series of text messages to attend without him.

He stepped into the bathroom to take a quick shower

and noticed her belongings set neatly on the vanity. Makeup, curling iron, facial wash and some other toiletries women used. Syd wasn't a girlie girl by any means but she did have a soft, tender side to her that he'd always been aware of despite her tough-girl personality. But in her field she had to be tough. However, he could sense her guard slowly coming down, and the last look she'd given him before he'd headed out was soft and delicate mixed in with the heated stare that he loved to see. It was the same look she'd given him when they'd finished their ride, and he'd pushed her against the wall to continue a different kind of invigorating adventure. Today it had appeared again, and he'd had to hold himself back from seizing her to him and releasing the pent-up desire he'd had since the day he had laid eyes on her across the courtroom five years ago.

Bryce quickly showered, threw on some jeans and a brown leather shirt and headed down to the meet and greet. He needed to see her eyes on him once more to make sure the look of promise and realization still blazed.

He scanned the huge ballroom for Syd among a sea of bikers clad in leather and jeans, tattoos and piercings. He spotted a few gentlemen he knew from different fests over the years; they approached him, and struck up a conversation. They were attorneys, as well, and he briefly told them about starting his own firm, but he wasn't interested in the conversation. Normally, he attended the meet and greet for networking purposes, but tonight his only mission was to find Sydney. He politely nodded and sipped on a glass of Hennessy as he excused himself and walked around the room.

"Damn, she's fine," he heard a man say.

Bryce pivoted in the direction of the voice and wasn't surprised to see Syd talking to another man a few feet away from the one who was ogling her. He gave the man a brusque look, and he immediately turned back around sheepishly to his circle of friends.

Bryce stared at the vision of loveliness before him. She was wearing a pair of black leather pants that insinuated her curvy hips and butt. Her hot-pink halter was tied around her neck and showcased her smooth back, which he wanted to run his hand and tongue along. Her bouncy hair moved along with her head as she laughed at whatever the guy was saying to her.

Couldn't be that damn funny, he thought. He downed the rest of his drink and slammed the glass on the nearest highboy. He approached the pair and made instant eye contact with Syd, who gave him the most beautiful smile he'd ever seen and then sighed with wide eyes and a pursed lip. Apparently, she was just trying to be nice to the annoying man who'd had too much to drink.

"Hey, what's up?" he asked, completely ignoring the guy.

"Hey, man," the guy started, placing his hand on Bryce's shoulder. "I'm talking to the little lady. We're about to go sightseeing on my hog."

Bryce turned to him, glancing down at the hand that rested on his shoulder and back at the guy, chuckling sarcastically. "You may want to remove your hand from me. Right now."

"And who are you? Her big brother? She'll be in good hands."

"Trust me—I'm not her big brother, and she's not going anywhere with you."

The guy dropped his hand from Bryce's shoulder and used it to pull Sydney to him.

"You need to let go of me," she said with authority. "I'm the wrong one to mess with."

The guy let go of her and stepped back. "Trick please. You ain't—"

Steam rose from Bryce, and he grabbed the guy by the collar. "What did you say?" he demanded roughly as his jaws tightened.

Sydney pulled on his arm. "Let's just go. He's a jerk."

"Man, I'm sorry. I didn't know she was taken. She said she didn't have a man."

Bryce dropped him to the floor and grabbed Sydney's hand, pulling her out of the ballroom into the foyer area where more bikers were convened and down an empty hallway.

Bryce marched back and forth as she leaned against the wall.

"Bryce…" she said in a calming, soothing tone. "I'm fine. It's no biggie. I deal with punks like him all the time. He really wasn't all that bad until you showed up."

"Syd, I wanted to beat him to a pulp."

She winced at his aggressive tone. "Well…thank you, but—"

He stopped pacing and stood in front of her. "Why did you tell him you didn't have a man?"

She twisted her lips to the side and stared up at him questionably. "Um…because I don't."

He grabbed her to him, his chest still heaving up and down with anger from the guy touching Syd and calling her a name.

"Who did you come with?" he whispered on her lips through clenched teeth.

She licked her lower lip, her eyes shooting off the fervor he longed to see. "You," she said breathlessly. "I came with *you*."

She captured his lips with hers, kissing him deeply as her tongue unleashed an untamed dance on his. He pulled her by the hips and meshed her body against his, causing low purrs to erupt from her throat. His erection strained against his boxers, wanting to break free. Wanting to join with her once and for all. Stumbling them back against the wall, she ran her hands in his dark, curly hair and down to his face as their kissing intensified. No woman had ever rocked him like this. He'd never craved a woman, but Sydney was like no other he'd ever met. The connection had always been there, even when she'd despised him and didn't know the true him. There was a longing for him he could see in her eyes and now feel on his lips as she granted him feral kisses in public as bikers passed by with whistles and catcalls. She'd driven him crazy for years, and now he wanted to drive her mad all night.

She pulled away from him, her luscious breasts heaving up and down. She ran a hand along his face and scooted from his embrace. *Shoot, not again*, he thought.

Bryce stared after her as she slowly strode away from him, her hips and butt swaying back and forth. She turned around with a puzzled expression.

"Aren't you coming?"

Chapter 8

Sydney didn't know what had gotten into her, but she was enjoying every single moment of it. She'd wanted him desperately, and after Bryce had stood up for her with the drunken jerk, she desired him even more. The long, crowded elevator ride was torture, especially with him pressed behind her, his arms encircling her waist and his erection hard on her backside. She was grateful when they made it to their floor, and she hurriedly rushed to their room while he lagged behind. Sydney glanced over her shoulder to see what was taking him so long. He wore a dark, seductive expression that jolted pure ecstasy wildly through her.

She made it to the door first. In her haste to leave the room earlier, she'd forgotten the key card on the nightstand. She leaned on the door as Bryce approached, and he pulled her into his arms and kissed her deep and hard. His hand reached past her as he touched the key card to the lock and pushed open the door while his lips never left hers. Stumbling them inside, he shut the door with his foot and glided her against the wall. His tongue traveled down her neck, provoking moans from her as she furiously unbuttoned his shirt. Shaking out of it, he moved his hands to her face, bringing his lips to hers once more with soft tender kisses, nibbling on her bottom lip and teasing her tongue with his.

"You're too sexy—you know that?" he said against her mouth.

Pushing him to the opposite wall in the foyer, she stood back admiring his magnificent sculptured chest. He was defined like a Greek god, with tight brown muscles that she couldn't wait to run her tongue across. Reaching her hand back, she untied her halter, letting it fall around her shoulders and down her body, exposing her breasts.

"Succulent. Juicy. Ripe." He licked his tongue over his bottom lip and stepped forward. "My kind of melons."

"Be patient," she whispered, even though she didn't know how much more patience she had left. "You'll get to them and me soon enough."

She slipped the shirt over her head and stepped out of her heels. Next she unbuttoned and unzipped her pants and eased them over her hips and off her body. He watched with a heated glare; her eyes never wavered from his. Approaching him, she glided her hands up his washboard abs to his chest and placed a sensual kiss to his neck. Licking and taunting it, causing purrs of delight to escape her throat. He ran his hands down her waist and to her hips, teasing the waistband of her white lace panties that were apparently in his way because he yanked them down. He lowered his head and tugged on one of her nipples, making it hard and taut as he kissed and licked it, going back and forth between the two, while squeezing them gently with his hands.

His mouth sought hers once more in a whirlwind kiss, triggering fire to rupture throughout her body, and only Bryce could extinguish it. After lifting her, he carried her to the bed and laid her down on it. Standing by the edge, he unzipped his jeans and slid them and his boxers down.

Grasping the pillow, Sydney gulped at the beautiful view in front of her. She sat up on her knees to meet his lips as he leaned over to kiss her and bring her close to him. Pulling him on top of her, she intertwined her legs around his trim waist as he ravished her lips and neck back and forth as if he couldn't decide where he wanted his lips. He sank farther down, gliding his tongue to her breasts, putting his entire mouth around her nipple as her moans filled the air. The warmth of his hard body on hers sent waves of tingles over her, and the need to be one with him increased with each passing second. She grasped the pillow again as his tongue drove lower, circling her belly button as his hands slid back up to grasp and knead her breasts.

Sydney didn't know passion could be so free and

feral, but his lips and hands were driving her crazy and wreaking emotions on her she'd never experienced. He sat up, bringing one of her legs with him. Massaging the erogenous points on her foot, he kissed her leg softly, traveling down inch by inch until he reached her inner thigh. She was already trembling with anticipation, but when he gently kissed the spot between her thighs, she shot all the way up and clutched his shoulders. He twirled his tongue around her clit and moved to the other thigh, lifting that leg in the air and trailing kisses upon it until he reached her foot. Taking both legs, he sat her feet on his left shoulder and massaged her erogenous points. Sheer excitement shot through Sydney's veins as sounds of pleasure escaped her and the trembling of her body scared her for a moment, it was all new and surreal.

Parting her legs so that one foot rested on each shoulder, Bryce dived his body between her until his lips were on hers again in an untamed kiss that was full of what was still to come, and she welcomed it. She glided her hand down his chest until she reached what she was seeking, but he held her hand to the mattress.

"Be patient."

"But I want it now." She tried to remove her hand from under his, but he held it firm.

"Soon. I'm not done driving you crazy."

His lips crashed onto hers once more but this time slower, taking his time as their tongues rotated together. He left her mouth as a questioning moan escaped, and he winked, sliding his body down hers as his tongue teased her clit once more. She hoped this time he would stay put and stop playing with her. He dipped lower, circling his tongue wildly, leaving no spot untouched. The pleasure rippled through, multiplied with each stroke, and she quivered violently, unleashing sounds and curse words from her throat she didn't even know existed. The man was a mastermind at his craft and should teach classes on how to give a woman an orgasm just from the caress of his tongue.

Okay, so maybe she was wrong about earth-shattering orgasms simply not existing. Apparently, they did, but no one before had ever created such a glorious rush of pure delight and bliss within her. After climbing out of the bed, Bryce disappeared into the bathroom, then returned carrying a box with one of its contents already over his erect rod.

"When did you buy those?"

He pulled her legs to him, wrapping them around his waist.

"Today, before I came back up to get dressed for the meet and greet."

"Glad you read my mind," she said, resting her hands on his neck.

He kissed her forehead and eased in the tip, rolling it around the opening before sinking it in as a relieved gasp escaped her. He continued slowly as they merged together as one. He stayed still for a second while she shifted to get used to his size. He began stroking slowly, going in and out at a steady pace. The sensations from earlier were returning, and she began to raise her hips up to meet his thrusts, which sped up. Raising her legs over his shoulders, he held her hands to the mattress as their lovemaking intensified. Bolts of passion raced through her as his dominant strokes rocked her to the core. The orgasm that transpired was the most unbelievable force of power she'd ever experienced and more magnificent than she'd deemed possible.

Intertwining his hands in her hair, Bryce kissed her tenderly as their pace slowed to a comfortable one. She was still having aftershock tingles between her thighs.

"You made the most beautiful faces and music," he said, nibbling her ear. "Can't wait to see and hear it again."

"If I have any left in me," she answered breathlessly.

"I'm sure you do."

And she did, over and over until he violently shook against her with a strong release of his own.

They lay together for a while in silence as their breathing returned to normal. He left her momentarily to bring her a bottle of water and turn the air conditioner up to full blast. He gathered Sydney in his arms, and she rested her head on his chest. Bryce's embrace was the safest place on earth, and she never wanted to leave it.

He kissed her forehead. "Did you ever think in a million years you and I would be lying here naked and completely satisfied after round one of lovemaking?"

"No. Um…round one?"

Sitting up, he gave her a cocky grin. "You can't handle another round?"

"What are you on? Viagra?" she teased.

He popped her butt and flipped her over, pinning her hands to the mattress. "Yep. You."

She laughed and then surprised him by flipping him over. "I can go all night, Counselor!" She reached over to the nightstand and grabbed a gold-wrapped packet from the box.

"I don't think your stamina can match mine."

"Boy, please. I've chased down criminals for blocks. I'll be fine." She rolled the condom down on him and then eased herself onto him. He grabbed her hips, but she took his hands and held them to the mattress. "I'm on top. I'm in control." She lowered her head and kissed his neck.

"For now," he said, closing his eyes with a sensual moan as she bestowed kisses along his neckline.

The feel of him under her was invigorating, just like a motorcycle ride but even better. As she sped up, he grasped her hips, bringing her farther down onto him, causing loud moans to elicit from her. She stared down at him as a naughty grin crossed his face while he continuously drove her mad with his thrusts reaching up to meet hers. They climaxed together moments later. She fell on top of him, completely sated and drained.

"Damn, girl! You gonna have the hotel calling the police on us," he teased, patting her bottom.

She sat up and rolled off him. "Was I that loud?" she whispered.

He laughed. "Now you want to be quiet. No, I'm just teasing. I love the fact you had a wonderful time and expressed yourself." He reached up and tenderly stroked her face. "That was the whole idea."

"I think you enjoyed yourself, as well," she said, kissing the palm of his hand before staggering out of the bed. "I'm going to take a quick shower."

"Can you walk straight?" he asked as she stumbled into the bathroom.

"I'm good," she answered as upbeat as possible despite the fact that her entire body felt as if she'd exercised all day. However, it was well worth it.

Bryce strolled into the bathroom and headed toward the bathtub.

"Take a good warm soak in the tub." He turned on the water and jets. "Afterward, I'll give you a body massage."

"Cool. You know what? You snatched me out of the meet and greet so fast I never had a chance to eat. Can we go grab a bite?"

"Can we compromise on room service?"

She eased herself into the tub as it filled up. "Room service is so overpriced, and they have the surchar…" She stopped as he stood there with an I-got-this expression.

He leaned over and kissed her deeply. "I'm going to take a quick shower and then order something from the menu." He skipped out of the bathroom and reentered with the room service book. "Look through it and let me know what you want when I get out. Glance at the bottled wine selection, as well."

An hour later, they sat on the couch, eating and sipping on red wine. She wore the shirt Bryce had on earlier that day unbuttoned while he lounged in one of the hotel's thick terry cloth bathrobes that he'd ordered for both of them. She preferred to wear his shirt because she felt as if she were still in his warm embrace.

She dug her fork into the chicken parmesan dish while glancing back and forth at Bryce. He'd finished his steak and baked potato and sipped his wine as he watched her eat.

"You're going to keep staring at me?" Heat rushed into her cheeks and she lowered her head. She couldn't believe how he was gazing at her.

"Can't help it. You're beautiful and glowing." His words were laced with sex, and she knew where they'd end up and it wasn't in dreamland.

"Well, we did just have earth-shattering sex," she answered, sipping her wine and scooting closer to him on the couch.

He reached out and pulled her onto his lap, kissing her tenderly. "That we did. Can't wait until we do so again."

He nuzzled her neck, and she giggled as his facial hair prickled along her skin. "We have the rest of the weekend."

"And what about after the weekend?" he asked seriously, taking a sip of his drink.

She tapped his hard pecs with her index finger. "What's that Vegas saying?"

He'd seemed somewhat taken aback. "So you want to leave it here?"

"Sure…I mean, we're obviously sexually attracted to each other, and it was definitely some type of wild, passionate journey to seduction on both our parts. However, don't worry, I'm not one of those women who has sex with a man and reads something more into it. We're having fun, and I know how to leave it here."

He trailed his finger along her cheek. "Well…I guess we have three more nights full of fun and hot, wild sex. I may need to buy some more condoms."

Sydney shook her head. "No need. I bought the exact same ones from the gift shop while you were in the business center."

She stood and grabbed the tray of chocolate-covered strawberries with a bowl of whipped cream in the middle of them.

"Now…what are we going to do with these?"

Chapter 9

Sydney shot all the way up in the bed, but her head was heavy from a hangover, and she crashed back down against the fluffy pillows. Then she remembered she didn't have much to drink the preceding night. Instead, she was hungover from Bryce. Reaching out to the other side of the bed, she felt nothing but empty space, but it was warm, which meant he hadn't left too long ago. It was pitch-black in the room except one little slit between the curtains. She sat up again, this time slowly, and hopped out of the bed, making her way to peek outside. The sun was definitely out, and she was grateful for the room's blackout curtains.

The bathroom door squeaked open, and she twirled to see Bryce in the doorway, beautifully naked, brushing his teeth. He was a fine specimen of a man with smooth mahogany skin that had moved along her caramel skin all night.

He held his index finger up and disappeared back into the bathroom. She trekked over toward him as he finished swishing and rinsing his mouth.

"Good morning, babe." He pulled her toward him, and she rested her head on his rock-hard chest. "Sleep well?"

"I could use a few more hours. Are you always this chipper in the morning?" she asked, pulling away and grabbing her toothbrush and toothpaste.

"You are definitely not a morning person."

Her sarcastic laugh filled the air. "Nope. I need coffee first."

He laughed and popped her butt. "Love the way it jiggles." He stood behind her and encircled his hands around her waist, placing a kiss to her shoulder.

"Are you going to watch me brush my teeth?" she asked. "This could get messy."

"I like messy." He kissed the crook of her neck tenderly, eliciting a soft moan from her. "Last night got kinda messy."

"Luckily, I was able to lick up all of the whipped cream." She wiggled her butt on his erection that had wedged itself between her cheeks. "All right now. We're supposed to be downstairs in an hour so we can head out to the track."

"Nervous?"

"Nope. I know the potential of Pretty in Pink. She'll be fine," she answered.

"Can't believe you signed up for this competition," he said, looking at her through the mirror. "There's going to be a lot of mean hogs out there."

"I can handle it." She shrugged. "I handled you last night, didn't I?" she asked with a wicked grin.

"Yes, you certainly did." He bit the side of her neck and slid his hands away from her. "Going to get dressed. I ordered breakfast for us when I got up, including a pot of coffee for you."

"Perfect."

He stepped out as she went ahead and brushed her teeth. When she was finished, she rushed out of the bathroom to find him on the couch with his laptop. Leaning over, she kissed him deeply. Sliding the laptop to the couch, he pulled her on top of him, unleashing his enticing tongue around hers.

She lifted her head and pulled away from him, but he playfully yanked her back down. "Where you going?"

"Bryce, I came to give you a good-morning kiss. I just wanted to make sure I'd brushed my teeth first. Going to hop in the shower."

He released her and slid his laptop back onto his thighs. "You know I can get used to your good-morning kisses," he said seriously.

She laughed it off as she closed the bathroom door and leaned against it. While she enjoyed waking up to him and being playful, they had to stick to their agreement from last night. There was no getting used to anything between them. Sleeping in his arms had been one of the best nights of her life. She'd been warm and cozy

nestled against his chest. During the night, he stirred
in his sleep and planted a few sweet kisses on her neck.
She loved the gesture, but she had to keep telling herself
not to get too comfortable with him. Their relationship
was strictly sex and only while they were in Vegas. The
thought of that made her a little sad, but she shook it off
and hopped into the shower. She had to stay focused
on winning the race, but all she could think about was
making love to Bryce.

After breakfast, they headed down to the parking lot
to retrieve their bikes to jet to the track.

She slid up on her bike and leaned over seductively.
"Are you sure you don't want to ride behind me?" she
asked, giving him her best sex kitten smile.

"As appealing as that is, I'm not riding a pink bike.
Besides, we've never ridden together like this before.
Could be fun." He put on his helmet and straddled his
motorcycle. "Follow me." He dropped his visor and
backed out of the space.

She nodded and placed her helmet on. She revved
up her engine and kicked up the kickstand. She gave
the go signal, and he zoomed off with her following.
There were other bikers headed down to the Las Vegas
Motor Speedway. It was about a fifteen-mile trek, but
Bryce had prewarned her they should just cruise and
not show off considering a lot of the bikers on the way
would be racing, as well.

Once they arrived, Syd registered and placed the
number given to her on the back of her jacket. There
were quite a few different races that day. Syd had only

entered one since she'd decided at the last minute to go and most of the other slots were already filled. So she'd signed up for the three-lap race for women. She just had to stay in her, lane which would be hard to do. She loved to drive fast, and, thanks to her training, she knew how to weave in and out of other motorcycles safely.

Bryce pulled her onto his lap as they sat in the stands watching the races below. There were two more before it was her turn, and she was told to be ready during the one right before hers. Bryce was being such a sweetheart, rocking her back and forth and rubbing her back. *A girl could get used to this*, she thought. However, she pushed it aside because that wasn't going to happen. They were just going to have fun in Vegas and then return to Atlanta without looking back.

Thirty minutes later, she headed down to the designated area. She'd already parked her bike there as instructed earlier, and she hopped up on it, holding her helmet and gazing into the stands to find Bryce, but she didn't see him. Her eyes perused the area where she'd left him and there was still no sign. She figured he went to the restroom or to grab something to snack on at the concession stand. She was completely surprised at herself for being so concerned as to where he was. He wasn't her man, but at least while they were there he was, and she wanted his nod of encouragement before the race began.

Her cell phone vibrated from the inside pocket of her jacket. She unzipped and reached into it to read the text. She'd avoided contacting Megan or any other family members since she had arrived in Vegas except to say she'd gotten there safely. She was hoping her recent text wasn't one of them.

She glanced at the text message as a wide smile inched across her face. She read it in his sexy, deep voice that he always seemed to use with her recently.

Turn around.

There he was on the side of the track, wearing a delicious smile on his ruggedly handsome face. She was sure her grin matched his if not wider.

Can you believe I'm actually nervous?

Man up, woman!

LOL!

She shook her head at him and placed her cell phone back in her pocket when the speaker announced through a bullhorn that they would begin in five minutes and to head to the starting line. She cast one more look at Bryce, who yelled out, "You got this!"

Giving him two thumbs up, she shut her visor and headed to the starting line.

There were eight other women racing, as well, but Sydney wasn't concerned about them. This race would be a piece of cake. She listened as the announcer read out the rules, and she concentrated on waiting to hear the gun go off.

When it did seconds later, she shot off, as did the other bikers as they all sped down the track. Some were neck and neck while a few lagged behind. She couldn't hear the cheers and wasn't really concerned because her focus point was zooming around the track again so she could see Bryce standing on the sidelines cheering her on. When she made it around the first time, she was in third place. Her eyes caught a quick glance of his manly physique, and she sped up, passing the woman in second. She was almost about to pass the woman in first, but Syd held back until the last part of the third lap. The ladies were neck and neck. The other biker passed Syd but only for a second. Her goal came into view and the words Bryce had shouted earlier played in her head like a broken record, and she zoomed past the other woman and through the ribbon first. She slowed down and parked on the side as Bryce came running toward her, lifting her off the motorcycle and twirling her in his comforting embrace and screaming at the top of his lungs.

"I knew you'd do it! That's my girl! They ate your dust!"

He continued with some other compliments as she laughed, but she really didn't care about winning. She was elated just to be in his arms.

The other bikers congratulated her, and the announcer presented her with a trophy.

They watched a few more of the events, which were mostly performed by professionals riding their bikes over cars or jumping off ramps and doing other tricks with their motorcycles. Afterward, they headed back, had dinner at a buffet and gambled in the casino. They returned upstairs around midnight after having won six hundred dollars between them, which Syd threw on the bed and laid on top of.

He picked some of it up and tossed it on her. "You do realize we broke even? We really didn't *win*." He laid down next to her and pulled her close to him. She rested her head on his chest and tried to shut out the countdown that played in her mind of when they'd be back in Atlanta and back to their normal lives, minus the bickering and bantering.

"Yeah, but at least it wasn't a total loss. I can't afford to lose my hard-earned money, especially if I'm contemplating leaving the GBI soon."

"So you're serious about taking the bar?"

"I might as well take it." She sat up and leaned against the pillows. "I can study for it while I'm off and, like you said, do some soul-searching." She let out a big yawn. "It's been such a long day. I just want to take a shower." She scooted off the bed and headed to the bathroom.

She closed the door and threw off her clothes and grabbed her shower cap off the vanity.

A tap at the door sounded, and she opened it to see Bryce in his boxers with his hands behind his back. "Can I join you?" he asked with a sly fox smile.

She ran her hand down his chest. "Of course, Counselor."

Sydney proceeded to turn on the shower and let the

water heat up before she stepped in. She was surprised when he didn't follow her. She glanced over at him leaning against the counter still wearing the same smile and his boxers.

"I thought you were getting in?"

"I'll just watch for a moment."

"Suit yourself." She grabbed the shower gel from the shelf and the washcloth from the towel rod and lathered up. She glanced over at him again. He'd now stepped out his boxers as his friend sprung forward at full attention. He swiped something from the counter, but it was still behind him.

"Can you wash my back?" she asked, curious to know what he was hiding.

"Sure." He stepped forward and opened the glass shower door. She handed him the washcloth and shower gel. Out of the corner of her eye, she saw him set the gold packet on one of the soap shelves. He scrubbed her back in a rotating motion before sliding the washcloth around to her chest and lowering his lips to her neck. Moaning, she reached her mouth around to his. He meshed his body tightly against hers and wandered his hand between her legs, slipping a finger inside, but their kissing never missed a beat. His erection was strong and hard on her butt, and she wiggled against him, wanting so bad for it to replace his finger. She turned around and faced him, placing kisses on his chest and twirling her tongue around his nipple.

"That feels so good, babe."

"I know something else that will feel even better," she said, handing him the packet.

She kissed him softly at first, trying to memorize the feel of his lips so she would never forget them after Vegas. She pulled his head down to her deeper as he delved his tongue into her mouth in a sensual assault that amplified every time their tongues met, and her moans grew louder. He turned her so she was in the corner of the shower under the water flow but not quite getting wet.

She wrapped one of her legs around him and kissed him with more aggression. He lifted his head and trailed kisses along her neck and down to her breasts, pulling and biting them.

"Bryce, baby...you... That feels so good." She clutched his shoulders as one of his hands massaged her entire feminine area, unleashing shivers throughout her. Squeals erupted from her. She found herself under the shower, but he pulled her back to the corner.

"I don't want your hair to get wet."

She ripped the shower cap from her head and threw it down. "I don't care." She panted breathlessly, pulling them directly under the water stream. "I really don't care."

He ripped open the packet as she placed kisses along his neck and ears. He lifted her leg higher around his waist.

"Hold on to me tightly," he demanded, entering her in one thrust.

Circling her arms around his neck, she nibbled his

bottom lip. "Yes, Counselor." She began to meet his thrusts over and over. He held on to her tightly as his muscular arms surrounded her in a warm cocoon. She felt secure with him even when he picked her up, and she wrapped both of her legs around his waist. Sydney knew he wouldn't drop her as he slid her up and down on him at a fast pace while their kisses matched. After unlatching her lips from his, she leaned her head back as an orgasmic rush hit her and she trembled in his arms.

"Bryce…keep going. Baby, please," she begged, which was so unlike her, but she didn't care. Being joined with him was so intense and emotional that for a second she thought she could actually fall for him.

"I got you, babe." He pulled her with him to the shower seat as she continued the roller-coaster ride she was on. He weaved his fingers into her wet hair as their mouths touched, but they didn't kiss as she sighed and moaned with each passionate stroke. He stared at her with heated eyes that she found herself falling into the more they continued their passionate tryst. He'd been right. Sex was so much better than riding a motorcycle. She'd just never had the right man with so much stamina and vigor before. Now she didn't know how she was ever going to be without this feeling of ecstasy.

Bryce's vibrations began to pick up as she slammed harder on him, and she knew his release was near. He grabbed her bottom and squeezed it tightly as he shivered inside her.

"Ahhhh…Syd…damn girl…uhhh," he yelled out as

she felt his warmth pulsating inside her. She clenched her muscles around him to make him tremble.

"You good, babe?" she asked, wiping the sweat from his brow.

"Do you have any idea how much power you have between your legs?"

She grinned mischievously and clenched herself around him again just to see an aftershock tremble. "Yep."

He chuckled. "What am I going to do with you?" he asked, lifting her off him. She settled on the shower seat.

"You can regain your strength, and we can go one more round in a few." She stood and turned off the water.

"Let's finish this in the bedroom," he said gruffly, opening the shower door and stepping out first. He took her hand, then surprised her by flinging her over his shoulder as she laughed hysterically.

On Sunday they attended the closing events, including a desert bike ride and a few workshops on how to do tricks on a motorcycle. That evening, they attended a superstar's show that was in residence at the casino next door.

After they made love Sunday night, she rested her head on Bryce's chest, thinking about the next two days traveling back to Atlanta. He rubbed her back before he fell asleep, and that was one of the many little things she would miss. He was always caring and thoughtful, even if their newfound friendship was solely based on sex. At least they'd been able to get out their pent-up frustrations with each other and parlay it into a friendship where they would no longer argue. However, she sort of liked that part, considering he was so sexy and commanding when he was angry.

The next morning, they finished packing in silence. She didn't know what to say to him since once they left Vegas behind, that was it. He'd been quiet and somewhat reserved during breakfast except for a few phone calls about Mrs. Thomas's situation. Sydney called the bellhop, and the same one who'd brought their luggage up upon their arrival showed up ten minutes later with a cart. Bryce helped him load and Sydney walked around the room one more time, making sure they didn't leave anything. She had a habit of leaving shower gel or a sock behind. "I called down to valet to have them bring around the Range and the trailer. Then I'll load up the motorcycles. You want to wait in the lobby, and I'll come get you when I'm out front?"

"Um…sure." She'd barely heard what he'd said. She was in such a daze. Their fun had come to an end.

"Cool." He pulled some money out of his wallet and scribbled something on the notepad on the desk and left it there with the money.

"Come on, young man," Bryce said, patting the bellhop's back "You can finish telling me about your golf lessons this weekend and your plans for grad school."

After they left, Sydney glanced at the note and the

cash. It was a four-hundred-dollar tip for the maid service. She smiled, grabbed her purse and gazed around the room one last time.

Chapter 10

Bryce pulled into Sydney's driveway a little after nine on Tuesday night. They'd had a nice trip back and managed not to discuss what had transpired between them in Vegas as they'd agreed. He had found safe topics to discuss in order to avoid it even though all he could think about was her warm, sensual body naked under on top of and on the side of him.

He was disappointed she hadn't mentioned their tryst. It was truly as if it had never happened for her, though he did sense her guard coming back up. Especially when she didn't take her shades off until the last drop of sunlight had completely vanished. He didn't remember her wearing them in Vegas. They'd rested in her hair the majority of the time. He'd thought perhaps they'd share a suite again, but she made her own hotel reservations for the journey back.

He turned off the engine and rested his hands on the steering wheel. "I'll take your bike off the trailer and park it in the garage."

She dug around in her purse and pulled out the remote for her garage, as well as the key to her motorcycle.

"Okay. I'm going to grab my suitcase and ice cooler from the backseat."

"I got it."

"Thanks. I'll meet you inside."

Twenty minutes later, he found her sitting on her couch going through mail and tossing the majority of it on the floor.

"Pretty in Pink is secured in the garage." He tossed the keys on the coffee table and glanced up at the roses on her fireplace mantel. He was surprised she hadn't thrown them away considering they were pretty much dead. The coolness of her home had helped them stay alive a little longer.

"So you need a ride to pick up your car tomorrow?" he asked.

She looked somewhat startled at his question but shook her head. "Nope, Stan is sending one of his boys to pick me up or I can take the bus. Aren't you going to check on Mrs. Thomas in the morning?"

"Yep, and I have an interview with an attorney who is interested in being a partner. Cool cat. We've played golf together for years, and we've always joked we should open a practice together."

"That's awesome. I'm sure everything will work out for you." She yawned and stretched. "Excuse me. It's been a long past few days."

"Yes, it has, but I've enjoyed hanging with you and getting to know you… All of you."

She laughed but still managed to avoid complete eye contact with him. "Me, too." She stood. "I'll walk you out. Text me when you get home."

He wasn't ready to go yet, but he knew they had to say goodbye. "Will do." He pulled her into his arms and kissed her slowly, savoring her lips one last time. "You want me to spend the night…you know, get it out one last time?" He didn't have any more condoms, but he'd run to the store around the corner if she said yes.

"Uh-uh-uh," she said, pointing her finger at his chest. "We left that in Vegas, but I promise you I'll never forget it." She reached up and returned the kiss before releasing herself from his embrace.

Sydney walked him to the front door. He ran his palm down her cheek and to her hand, squeezing it before bringing it to his lips and kissing it tenderly. "I'm very glad we got to know each other on another level, and while we agreed to leave the intimacy part of our relationship in Vegas, I truly hope we'll remain friends."

"Yes, of course. I definitely agree. You're a great guy, Bryce. I'm glad we got to know each other, as well." She finally rested her eyes on him, and the same passion he'd seen in them during the trip remained.

"Sweet dreams, Syd," he said, kissing her forehead and strolling to the car.

Bryce wasn't going to let her get away this easy. While she may have thought what they had would remain in Vegas, she was sadly mistaken. They may have completed one journey, but now it was time for another, except this time he wasn't letting her go. He was going to give Sydney Chase the *chase* of her life.

It was the day after Sydney's return from Vegas. Surprisingly, when her alarm went off at seven o'clock in the morning, she actually got out of bed and opened the blinds. She'd grown accustomed to the early-morning sun while hanging with Bryce. So when the phone rang punctually at eight o'clock, she was sort of hoping it was him as she ran and slid on her bed to grab the cell from the nightstand. But it was Stan from the auto shop letting her know he was sending someone to pick her up because her car was ready.

After everything was squared away with her car, she headed to the shooting range. When the phone rang again she hoped it was Bryce, but alas it was Megan. She pushed the button on her earpiece so she could keep her hands on the wheel.

"Hey, Syd," Megan said. "Glad you're back. We need to discuss the final plans for our thirtieth birthday party this Saturday."

"Good to be back. So what else is there to discuss?

I thought it was a casual, intimate dinner with family and close friends at your home." She could only imagine what Megan had planned.

"It is, but the caterer called and wanted to know the final guest count. I received your email, and we pretty much have the same list considering we're inviting close family and friends in the city. Is there anyone else you wanted to add before I call her back? A plus one perhaps?"

Syd thought about Bryce. Of course he would be there since Megan invited him to everything. If she had to add a plus one, it would've been him. But she reminded herself that they decided not to pursue anything further.

"Nope. No plus one. Is Bryce going to be there?" She couldn't believe she'd asked that out loud and really wanted to retract her last statement. She never asked Megan about Bryce and hoped her sister wouldn't realize that.

"No. I didn't invite him."

"Why not? You always invite him to family gatherings." *Okay, I gotta stop talking.*

"Because you two only argue, and we don't want bickering at our birthday party. It's supposed to be a happy day."

"True, but he is Steven's brother. I know how to avoid him. I did so at your anniversary party a few months ago."

"Yeah, surprisingly, but there were so many people at Braxton's club, you weren't even in the same vicinity. I'll go ahead and invite him, though. I did feel bad about not telling him. He's such a great guy, and I'm so happy I suggested that he hire Tiffani for the tutorial workshop at the community center on Saturdays. She needed the extra money."

"So I heard," Sydney said, exiting off the interstate.

"From whom? Tiffani said she hadn't spoken to you in a few weeks."

Oh, shoot, Sydney thought.

"Oh, um…she mentioned needing extra money for something she was saving for. This was a while back."

"You know I was thinking about hooking Tiffani up with someone. It has been a few years now since Keith passed and even though KJ has his grandfather, Tiff's brother and of course Steven, maybe it's time she settled down with someone. She's starting to date again but she's so picky and says she'll never marry again but wouldn't mind having a companion. What do you think, sissy?"

Sydney snickered. "I think I find it odd that this is coming from the person who hated all the blind dates me and Tiffani set up for her years ago. Now you want to return the favor?"

"Shall I add you to the list? Steven has a lot of nice friends and associates. At one point, I thought about Bryce for you, but you can't stand him. Oh, I know. I'll set him up with Tiffani. He did say she was a blessing to the program and a really sweet girl. Hmm…that could work."

Sydney's heart sank all the way to the floor mat of

her Mustang, and she slammed on the brakes when she realized the light was red. Luckily, no one was in front of or behind her.

Bryce and Tiffani would never work. Tiffani was the sweet, pretty third-grade teacher who saw everything through rose-colored glasses like a Disney princess. She was into arts and crafts, kiddie activities with her son, baking cupcakes and her flower gardens. Everything in her life was pretty and perfect. She wouldn't be caught dead on the back of a motorcycle, especially if she had to wear a helmet and mess up her waist-length thick hair that she made sure was in place no matter what. And she certainly wouldn't let Bryce do the kinky things he'd done to her in Vegas. While Tiffani wasn't a prude, whenever the word *sex* was brought up in a conversation, she'd wrinkle her nose and say she didn't talk about her and Keith's sex life. Of course, that had been when he was alive.

No, Sydney didn't see a match made in heaven between the two of them. Bryce was too much of a man's man for Tiffani.

"Mmm…I don't think they would work out, but I'm sure one of Steven's friends would be a good idea," Sydney answered, not believing there was a tinge of jealously in her mind. That wasn't like her at all. Bryce could date whomever he wanted. So could she. Her stomach twisted into a big tight double knot.

"Yeah, I suppose you're right. Bryce prefers more of a challenge. Did you run into him in Vegas?"

She and Bryce had agreed if anyone asked—which

she knew Megan would—that they would say they had bumped into each other briefly. Made a few cordial pleasantries and that was it.

"Yep, I saw him for a quick moment."

"Glad you finally went on a vacation. So back to the party plans. Just to clarify, you're fine with green pea soup, Waldorf and green salad, followed by beef brisket and salmon with the sides you selected. And for dessert crème brûlée and assorted cupcakes made by Tiffani."

"All this food talk is making me hungry," Sydney said as the time Bryce made breakfast for her popped into her head. "Think I'll stop off to breakfast some-place before I go to the shooting range."

"Well, enjoy the rest of your day. I'm going to head to the office. I have a meeting with a celebrity who wants all white everything for her penthouse. Thank goodness she's a neat freak and doesn't live in Atlanta full-time."

"Cool. Have fun."

After hanging up, Syd decided to skip breakfast and head straight to the shooting range. She wasn't really hungry. She'd had an apple and coffee before she'd left the house. Besides, she was anxious to get to the range. It released stress and kept her trained for her job. She rarely had to shoot a gun because of her position, but she always had to be prepared. Plus, she needed to re-lease some pent-up energy and the withdrawal she was having due to Bryce's absence. She'd heard of such a thing but had never experienced it. Her emotions were all over the place thanks to him. Luckily, when she arrived at the range her favorite booth was available, and she spent thirty minutes shooting off rounds from her gun as well as some other firearms available at the facility.

Taking her ear protectors off, she heard her cell phone beep from inside her purse. It was a text from Bryce about twenty minutes earlier.

Good morning. Just making sure everything is okay with your car.

Yes, it is. I'm at the shooting range.

Where are you headed afterward?

Home to eat.

How about I take you to lunch after my meeting, say around 11:30?

Sydney glanced at her watch. It was after ten o'clock. She glimpsed down at her Clarke Atlanta sweatshirt and old jeans with the hole in the knees. The ones that didn't come that way. They were worn-out. When Stan had called earlier about her car, she'd thrown on the first thing she'd grabbed from the drawer.

I'm not dressed.

Perfect. I like you like that.

Very funny. I meant for lunch, and I'm nowhere near home to change.

I don't care what you have on. Meet me at Tin Drum at Atlantic Station.

Okay.

She placed her ear protection back on and shot off more rounds. She couldn't believe she'd said yes to lunch. But they'd never agreed not to speak or hang out anymore. They'd decided no more sex since they got it all out of their systems in Vegas. However, she hadn't really, she thought as she reloaded and unloaded her gun two more times. Too bad she didn't drive her motorcycle. A nice long, hard ride was exactly what she needed to get it all out before she saw Bryce and jumped him in the Asian restaurant.

At a few minutes before the appointed time, she walked through the doors of Tin Drum. Her eyes zoomed on him right away speaking with another gentleman who had a take-out bag in his hand. As they stood near the bar Bryce was standing tall and handsome, exuding an essence of power and confidence. There were other businessmen in the place, but none of them had the same charismatic nature as he did. His presence outshone the others, along with his smile, charm and the delicious way his manly physique fit in the suit that more than likely was custom made for him. Her thoughts trailed to the day she'd first seen his bare chest and felt the beating of his heart on her breasts.

She'd never experienced such a connection with a man. Her body shivered and her pulse raced from just being in the same room with him. Of course, this was always what happened when she was near him. But it was usually because she was ready to give him her two cents on any given case. Or was it?

His eyes finally caught hers, and he smiled. Wide. Beautiful. Promising. She gulped and barely heard the hostess ask how many would be in her party. Bryce continued to chat with the other man, who, though handsome, wasn't Bryce. He wasn't the man she yearned for and who had kept her up last night tossing and turning with images of them making love embedded in her brain.

She followed the hostess to a booth and ordered a glass of water with no ice or lemon for the both of them. Bryce had finally shaken his associate's hand and moved her way.

He slid into his seat with his briefcase. "Hey. Sorry to keep you waiting. I ran into a friend of mine."

"No problem. He looks familiar."

"Broderick Hollingsworth, the real-estate developer and investor." He opened the menu and perused through it. "He's looking for a new attorney."

"Oh, I think I met him at the fund-raiser a few years back for the community center." Sydney opened her menu to the appetizers. "The one Megan arranged for Steven at Braxton's restaurant. That's the night they fell in love. That's how I remember it for she always says it."

"I remember that night, as well," he said with a twinkle in his eye. "We argued about a case I'd just won. You called me an ass and stormed away in your sexy stilettos, swishing those curvy hips of yours in a black dress. I remembered thinking if I just kiss her maybe she'd be quiet for once."

"Why didn't you?" she asked seriously with a raised eyebrow.

"Because you probably would've slapped me." He closed the menu and pushed it to the end of the table.

She laughed. "You're probably right."

After they ordered their food, Bryce opened his briefcase and took out a few books, handing them to Syd.

"These are some of the up-to-date books to help you study for the Georgia bar. And there's some information that I'll email you about classes and workshops you can take, as well, to help you prepare."

Sydney turned the pages of the book on top and became a little overwhelmed with all of it. She closed it, and set the books on the booth seat next to her purse. She groaned in her head. She'd woken up that morning ready to go back to work but then remembered she was on vacation for another three weeks. While she looked forward to the rest of her break, she wasn't sure anymore if she really wanted to study for the bar.

"Thank you. I'll look over all of it."

"Megan called earlier inviting me to your birthday dinner this Saturday. She said it was your idea," he mused with a cocky smile.

"I told her I'd behave. She didn't want you and me arguing on our birthday."

He nodded his head, stroking his goatee. The waitress dropped off their lunch along with a glass of juice for Bryce. He waited to respond until after the waitress left. Scooting his pad thai out of the way, he leaned in toward her. His eyes turned jet-black, holding her in a smoldering gaze.

"What if I don't want you to behave?"

She lowered her eyes as she tried to muffle a smile and twirled a noodle around on her fork. "We agreed that ended in Vegas." Even though now she was having second thoughts as she crossed and uncrossed her legs to ward off the tingling that arose just from his tempting stare.

"You know our families are going to find it weird that we aren't bickering, and we get along just fine now. What do you think we should do?"

"I honestly hadn't thought about it. It's not like we see each other except at family events and that's only, like, three or four times a year. We'll just keep it cordial."

He slid his plate back over and began eating. "Okay. Unfortunately, I can't stay too long, but I wanted to give you the material for the exam and to see your beautiful face."

"Bryce…" She couldn't believe she was actually blushing. She was sure of it since her cheeks were burning. She took a sip of her water to cool herself down.

"Just telling the truth. You do look in the mirror every day. Right?"

"Eat your food and stop drooling," she teased.

They continued the rest of their lunch, discussing his plans for the practice. Before long he had to run to a meeting with his accountant and left.

Sydney stayed to do some shopping since she was in Atlantic Station, an outdoor mall in the heart of midtown Atlanta. She rarely shopped for clothes unless she needed something in particular, and she decided to buy a new dress for her birthday dinner. She became increasingly frustrated with herself when she kept trying on things and deciding against them because she didn't think Bryce would like it. *Who cares what he likes*, she thought before settling on a peach dress with a flared skirt that ended right above her knees. It was fun, flirty and sexy, and for a moment she thought she was Megan when she looked in the mirror. She took it off and tried on another dress that was similar with a wraparound straight skirt and in the same color. *Much better,* she thought. They were identical in looks but not in style of dress. She put the other dress back on and took a picture for her sister and texted it to her.

Syd bought both dresses plus a few more things she needed. Her cell phone beeped in her purse twenty minutes later. It was Megan.

Love it! Please, pretty please get it for me. I can wear it Saturday.

Already bought it. Will drop off at your office since I'm near.

Thank you, sissy!

On the way home, Sydney thought about her dilemma with her career. Since being away from work, she didn't miss it because she needed the break to be able to clear her mind and think. Bryce had suggested she do some soul-searching while on vacation. However, now she had two things to think about, the other being Bryce. Her life was so much easier and simpler before she wound up in the hospital. Sure, she was exhausted at times, but a lot of that she brought on herself because she was the one who chose to work around the clock. Not Mumford. He was always the one telling her to go home and rest, but she never saw the point of going home because no one was there. She lived alone, and besides hanging out with her family and friends and the occasional date, work was her life.

Then there was Bryce taking her out of her normal routine of cuddling on the couch, eating pizza and watching classic movies. He actually cooked dinner, lit the fireplace, had a decent conversation and brought her coffee in the morning. If she was going home every day to something like that, then maybe she wouldn't work as much. Not that she wanted to go home to Bryce. She groaned and tapped her fingers on the steering wheel, shaking her head.

Okay, I'm just going insane because I'm almost thirty. That's all.

Sighing, she pulled into her garage, jumped out of the car, grabbed her helmet from a shelf and hopped on her motorcycle. She needed to ride and clear her head, yet the only thought in her brain was when she'd been wrapped safely in Bryce's embrace.

Chapter 11

Bryce arrived thirty minutes late to the birthday party for the twins. That wasn't his intent, but his meeting with another potential attorney ran longer than expected. He stepped into the foyer of his brother's lavish mansion not far from his own. Luckily, it was still cocktail hour and he hadn't missed the dinner. A party hostess took the gifts from him and set them on a table overflowing with bags and wrapped boxes for the birthday girls. He hadn't been sure what to give them. He'd thought about the exact same present but decided against it. They had similar yet different tastes, and he wanted them to love their gifts. He especially wanted to give Sydney something meaningful to her. He consulted Steven, who said Megan was almost out of her favorite perfume, Amarige, and for Syd, he bought a

Pandora charm bracelet with motorcycle and helmet charms. He felt it represented her sweet yet tough side.

Bryce's eyes sought out Syd. He spotted her chatting with one of Steven's golf buddies, Ross, near the grand piano, where Braxton was playing a jazz melody of songs. She was breathtaking in a straight peach dress that hit her curvy body in all the right places. Her hair was piled on her head, and her feet were encased in a pair of sexy stiletto sandals. His mind trekked to untying the tie around the skirt of the dress, unpinning her hair and pulling her legs around his waist but leaving the shoes on.

"What's up, baby brother?"

His older brother's greeting tore Bryce out of his fantasy, and he turned to see Steven in a red polo-type shirt and khakis. He handed him a glass of Hennessy and gave him a hug.

"Can't complain. How's Washington, Senator?"

"The same. We're going to start dinner in a few. Megan is around here somewhere delegating as if we didn't hire the caterer and a staff for a reason." Steven paused and raised his glass with a nod. Bryce turned to see Ross raising his glass with a knowing gleam in his eyes. Syd nodded and smiled, as well.

"Sooooooo what's going on with that?" Bryce asked, trying his hardest not to glance back over his shoulder. He couldn't hear what they were discussing because of the music, but he did hear Sydney's distinct laugh. A cute, flirty one. His chest muscles tightened.

"Oh, Megan thought it would be cool to introduce

them. She thinks Syd needs a man, and she thinks you need a woman."

"Ha, this coming from the person who didn't want any blind dates," Bryce said, taking a sip of his drink.

"Yeah, she thought about you and Tiffani together," Steven said, leading Bryce into the empty dining room. He really wanted to stay in the living room to eavesdrop on Ross and Sydney.

He shook the ice around in his glass and took a sip. "Mmm...sweet lady, great kid, but not my type. I need someone with a little more fire in her." His mind traveled to Sydney's blazing eyes and tough yet sweet personality. He wanted an even balance, and definitely not a girlie girl who wouldn't dare ride the back of his motorcycle.

"Yep. That's what I told Megan. So she did place cards," Steven stated, waving his hand across the long table that was set for twenty people. "The woman to your left is someone she wants you to meet."

"Oh, brother." Bryce chuckled. "I thought this was for close friends and family."

"Well, Stephanie, that's her name, is one of Megan's old friends from college. She just moved back into town. She's an attorney, too."

Moments later, Megan instructed everyone to enter the dining room and find their place cards. Bryce was elated that Syd was across from him a few seats down, with Ross on her left and Megan's best friend and business partner, Jade Whitmore, to her right. Megan had decided to place herself and Sydney in the center of the table since it was their birthday dinner, while their parents sat at each head. He was between Stephanie and Braxton. And while Stephanie was an attractive lady, she just didn't have that passion blazing in her eyes that he found alluring.

Bryce tried to make polite conversation with Stephanie while eating his split green pea soup. But she just wasn't his type, though she was intelligent and knowledgeable about the law. She'd recently passed the Georgia bar and was looking for a job. However, he couldn't focus on their discussion because one of his ears was burning with listening to Ross and Sydney's conversation. Well, it was mostly Ross speaking as Sydney sat there nodding and eating her soup. By dessert, Bryce was more tired than Sydney must be of listening to golf stories and Ross's political views. Some of which Bryce knew Steven wasn't in agreement with, but he liked how his big brother never pushed his political agenda on others.

He took a bite of his delicious turtle cupcake that Tiffani had made, grabbed his cell phone, set it in his lap and sent a text to Sydney.

Who's the lame guy you're with?

He watched Syd slide her phone off the table and glance at it, her facial expression never wavering.

You know Ross. He's a friend of your brother. So what about you and Stephanie?

She's cool. She's an attorney.

I know her. She's one of Megan's old friends.

Didn't you all go to college together?

Yeah, but we never got along.

So are you going on a date with this dude? I thought I heard him say something about golf lessons followed by dinner.

She placed her phone back on the table as her parents made a toast to her and her sister. And then the entire group sang "Happy Birthday" in unison.

Bryce downed his Hennessy and clenched his jaw, upset that she never responded to his text. Moments later, everyone made their way back into the living room with their dessert and coffee or after-dinner drinks. He noticed Syd take the back staircase alone. He dipped toward the front staircase and strode upstairs to see her disappear around a corner. Stepping up his pace, he caught the door of the bathroom before she closed it.

Her eyes were round like saucers as she quickly pushed the door shut and locked it "What are you doing here? Can I have some privacy please?"

"Wanted to talk to you alone."

"About what?" she asked with a twinkle in her eye. The profiler in her was obviously sizing him up.

He closed the gap between them. "You didn't answer my last text."

She smirked. "Oh, that. You jealous, baby?" she

asked sarcastically, taking her makeup bag from her purse and setting it on the counter.

"No. He's just not your type."

"Really?" She crossed her arms in front of her chest and tilted her head up to him. "And who *is* my type?"

He pulled her to him and kissed her, sinking his tongue in slowly before stepping it up a notch with zealous, wild kisses that she matched. He lifted her up onto the counter and slid his hand under her dress to her panties and glided a finger deep into her as she clutched his shoulders and let out a gasp.

"Shh…baby," he whispered on her lips, slipping in another finger, which caused another passionate gasp from her that he stifled with his mouth. He kept his eyes focused on her as she breathed against his mouth. Her head leaned back toward the mirror, and he placed tender kisses on her neck and down her cleavage, trailing back and forth as she wrapped her legs around his waist just as he'd imagined earlier. With his free hand, he untied the bow at her waist and the wraparound part of the skirt fell open, exposing her succulent thighs that he yearned to be in between. He lifted her head toward him and kissed her as her hips bucked against his fingers. He knew her release was near, and while her fervent moans were the best song he'd ever heard, everyone downstairs would hear, as well. His kiss became deeper as she quivered in his embrace and the panting on his lips intensified. As she calmed down, she glared at him with the fire he loved to see mixed with something wicked as she traveled her hand down to his slacks, unbuckled his belt roughly, zipped down his pants and pulled his erection out of his boxers. Stroking it hard up and down, she kissed him furiously, gyrating her tongue in his mouth and pushing him against the opposite wall.

"I thought you were going to behave?" he whispered teasingly.

"But you don't want me to. Remember?"

"Mmm…da…" He couldn't believe he sounded like a gibbering idiot, but her hands were massaging him just right.

"Shh…baby," she whispered seductively, lowering herself to the floor. She kissed the tip, licking it gently in a circle, and glided it into her warm mouth slowly as far as she could go, which wasn't all the way, but he didn't care. Her sexy, juicy lips engulfed him up and down. The soft pleasure moans she made in the back of her throat continued to drive him insane as she tightened her mouth around him. He placed his hands on her head, trying not to mess up her up-do while she ravished him. She glided back and forth, sometimes teasing the tip and then diving back, sinking him farther into her heated, wet mouth. Bryce tried to stand up straight and hold back the groan rising in his throat, but none of that happened as he slid down a tad on the wall. Sydney reached her hand up to his mouth to muffle him but didn't waver from the erotic session.

When she sped up, he reached around to his back pocket, pulled out his wallet and a gold-wrapped condom and opened it. He pulled her to her feet and pushed her back toward the counter, lifting her on it again. He brought her legs up to his shoulders, slid on the condom and in one push, delved all the way into her as far as he could go. She grasped his arms as he lowered his head to her mouth to silence both their moans and matched his kisses with his thrusts. Deep and hard. He'd never felt so connected to a woman. Everything about her was pulling him into her abyss of ecstasy. Her sweet smell. Her strength. Her smile. The way her eyes lit up whenever she looked at him. He no longer cared about their agreement. He had to make her all his.

She trembled in his arms, which meant her orgasm was near and so was his after the mind-blowing job she did earlier. Sliding her legs to around his waist to hold her better, he lifted his lips from hers as she let out a silent scream in the air all while keeping her eyes focused on his. Clutching her arms around his neck, her muscles clenched his manhood as she shook against him. He buried his head in her neck and held on to her for dear life as if she were a life buoy.

"Are you okay?" he whispered.

She nodded, and he backed way as she tied her dress back around her waist. He flushed the condom and zipped his slacks back up as she fixed her makeup and a few loose strands of hair that had fallen out of the hairpins. His arms encircled her waist, and he placed a gentle kiss to the back of her neck. He saw her beautiful glow through the mirror as his eyes caught hers in a penetrating stare.

He leaned down to her ear. "When is this shindig supposed to be over with?"

"Soon. Steven and Megan have to be at the private airfield before midnight. He has a fund-raiser brunch to attend tomorrow in DC."

Bryce glanced at his watch. "I'm leaving in thirty minutes. Follow me in ten. Come to my home so I can finish making love to you. I'll have the garage door up so you can just slide right in…like I plan to do later on."

She turned her head and kissed him provocatively, causing his manhood to stir again. He cleared his throat and slid his hands off her. She grabbed some tissue and wiped her lipstick off his mouth and neck. "I'll go back down first," he said, placing his hand on the doorknob.

She nodded, and he listened outside the door to make sure no one was in the hallway. They were in the guest quarters of the mansion so he didn't expect anyone up there considering there was a powder room downstairs. He opened the door, peeked out and made his way into the hallway as she closed the door behind him.

When he made it back downstairs, everything was still going on as it was twenty minutes ago. Braxton was on the keys and Megan was chatting with Tiffani and complimenting her on the cupcakes.

"Hey, bro. Where were you?" Steven asked, approaching him from his left.

"I had some business that needed handling."

Steven nodded. "So…how do you like Stephanie?"

"Mmm…thinking about seeing if she wants to interview for a job, but that's about it," he answered while glancing out of the corner of his eye as Sydney reappeared in the room. She joined Megan and Tiffani by the grand piano. He noticed Ross pull her to the side and from his wistful expression and Sydney's shaking of the head, she must've declined his golf date. Ross shook her hand and walked over to him and Steven.

"No love connection, huh?" Steven asked Ross.

"Nah, man. She said no."

Bryce rested his eyes on Sydney, who glanced his way. He rubbed his watch and walked over to grab another turtle cupcake. They were almost as addictive as Sydney. Thirty minutes later, he bid good-night to everyone and stated that he had a hot date.

Later on that night, his birthday girl lay in his embrace wearing nothing but the charm bracelet and an exhausted yet satisfied smile. She felt perfect in his arms. In his bed. In his home. In his world. Bryce wasn't going to rush her, but he damn sure wasn't going to beat around the bush, either.

Around two o'clock in the morning, he was awakened by a noise. He reached over to Syd but all he squeezed was a pillow and not her cute butt. In the dark, his eyes made out her silhouette in the shadow near the window putting on her dress.

He swung his legs out of the bed and sat on the edge. "Where are you going?" he asked gruffly.

"Home," she answered matter-of-factly.

"I'm not one of those men who kick women out after

a night of passion," he said teasingly. "You can stay for breakfast and past that if you want."

"I know, but I have to be up early in the morning and I need to change clothes. Can't wear this."

"Where are you going, if you don't mind me asking?"

"I do mind," she said in a brusque tone.

"Okay…"

She sighed. "I got a text from Mumford when you left the bathroom. I just need to go to the GBI office for a few hours to help with a case. That's all."

He flicked on the lamp next to the nightstand. "So you're going to start working around the clock again… on your vacation?"

"No. I told him I can only be there from nine to one. He was rather shocked yet pleased I gave a time. He was even more shocked when I told him I couldn't come right then. But Watkins was there and the kid is trying. He's just not as good as me."

"Well…it was your birthday dinner celebration, and you're on vacation."

"Mmm, that's not why I said no," she said plopping in the chair in the sitting area and slipping on her heels. "I've left events all the time early or arrived late. Work has always come first."

"Then why didn't you go last night?"

"Because I wanted to spend it with you," she said quietly.

He got out of the bed and kneeled in front of her. "I have some sweats and a T-shirt you can throw on. Just leave from here. I don't want you driving across town from Buckhead to Decatur at two in the morning. I'll make sure you get up in time. I'll even make sure you have some coffee. Okay?"

Sydney drove to the GBI office not believing she was in Bryce's sweats and T-shirt. Luckily for her they'd shrunk in the dryer, and he could no longer wear them. They were still a tad too big for her but she was comfortable. Very comfortable.

She couldn't believe she'd actually stayed the rest of the night. Being held in his secure embrace was soothing. His quiet snoring on her neck was peaceful, and he knew how she liked her coffee. That was a plus. When she'd opened the gift in the car before arriving at his home, she was quite surprised to see the charm bracelet. It reminded her of their time spent in Vegas. She glanced at it now on her wrist as the charms dangled from the pink leather band. It was definitely her. She didn't like a lot of flashy jewelry. She usually only wore a watch and a pair of diamond studs her parents gave her when she graduated from law school. After slipping the bracelet off her wrist, she placed it in her purse as she pulled into the parking lot of the GBI headquarters. Even though she worked with all men who didn't care about trinkets and whatnot, they would definitely notice if she wore a cute bracelet with a pair of sweats. That simply wasn't like her.

Her mind rewound to the fact that they hadn't managed to leave the sex part of their relationship in Vegas. She thought that would be much easier to do, and she reminded him when she left that it couldn't happen again. He'd simply nodded and shrugged as if it wasn't a big deal before laying a tender kiss to her forehead. She didn't know how long that was going to last, especially when he winked and curled his lips into a cocky grin as if it wouldn't be the last time. Sighing, she closed her thoughts on Bryce as she entered the building. She needed to place her focus on profiling the next creep who was breaking the law. However, she wasn't going to stay longer than the time frame she had given Mumford. While she was anxious to get back to work, she was enjoying her vacation and the realization of needing to change her habit of working around the clock. Thanks to Bryce, Sydney was beginning to understand what it meant to divide her time between her career and spending it with loved ones.

During the following week, Sydney focused on her things to do list that she'd created in the beginning of the year. But because of her busy work schedule, nothing had been checked off. Now she was able to tackle the tasks even though she hated to admit it was just a tactic to block her mind from thinking about Bryce. Luckily, he'd been busy with preparations of opening his practice. He'd called to tell her he'd closed on the building. She was happy about that but a little sad because all of his time would be spent with setting up the practice that he'd tentatively named Monroe and Associates.

By the middle of the week, Sydney had accomplished

majority of her chores and managed to do a little spring cleaning. She had closets full of stuff that she no longer needed. Some were useable and were going to a women's shelter. Everything else would be discarded.

After a much needed break, Syd threw the last trash bag in the overstuffed garbage can in the garage and opened the door to drag it to the edge of the driveway for tomorrow's pick up. While there, she checked her mail and flipped through a fitness magazine. A roaring engine boomed in her ear as she looked up and saw a motorcycle a few blocks down zooming her way. She tilted her head to the side as she recognized the helmet. He slowed down when he saw her and parked on the curb. It was a sleek motorcycle with two wheels in the back. She hadn't noticed it in his garage. He took off his helmet and showcased a dashing smile on his flawless brown face, and his jet-black curls glistened in the afternoon sun.

"Hey, beautiful." Bryce's eyes perused over her jeans and purple tank top. "I tried calling you. I didn't want to just drop over but the motorcycle dealership isn't far from here."

"No problem. I've been cleaning out closets and listening to music. I didn't hear the phone. Shouldn't you be somewhere working? Didn't you just close on an office building?"

"I think you've forgotten I can afford to hire people to take care of tasks for me. Megan has one of her interior decorators picking out office furniture and decorating the entire building. My main concern is hiring a competent set of attorneys."

The truth was she had forgotten about his wealthy background. She no longer saw him as the spoiled rich brat she had once thought he was. Instead, she was beginning to love everything about him and that scared her.

"How do you like my new motorcycle?"

She walked around it, giving a nod of approval. "I love it. When I can I drive it?"

"One day, but for now you can be the first passenger. Grab your helmet and lock your house up."

Ten minutes later, she wrapped her hands around his waist and pressed her legs against his. She gave the go signal and off they went.

Riding the back of a motorcycle had never been as exciting and satisfying as it was with Bryce. He was already a man's man, but he exuded even more power and control when on the motorcycle. She loved how he would speed up to tease her, and she'd pinched his waist to encourage him to slow down to a comfortable speed. He knew her limits and boundaries. She always had a sense of security with him. He wasn't a dangerous driver so he didn't weave in and out of cars, but if he saw a long stretch of road, he charged it.

Upon returning to her home, it began to rain so he thought it best to place the motorcycle in her garage to wait it out. He sat on it with his feet dangling over one side while she tossed some old paint cans and hard brushes into a garbage bag.

"What are all those bags lined up against the wall?" he asked.

"Clothes and some other things I'm donating to a women's shelter. I'm going to drop them off tomorrow before my lunch outing."

"Lunch outing?"

"Yes, with Megan and Tiffani. Megan is finally back in town but leaving again the day after tomorrow with Jade to shoot some scenes for their decorating show. Tiffani has a big announcement to make."

"Okay. I was going to ask you to stop by my new office to check it out."

"Tomorrow during the day won't be good at all. How about the evening?"

"Um…I have a business dinner meeting around seven." He stood up. "Seems like the rain has stopped."

"Yep." She hated hearing the tone in his voice that meant he was getting ready to leave, but she had to keep telling herself that they were just friends.

"I'm going to take this last bag to the street when you back out." She turned around to tie it shut with the yellow handles when she sensed Bryce directly behind her.

"You know you really shouldn't bend over like that, at least not in front of me."

She stood all the way up but didn't turn around. His hands moved along her waist and under her shirt, traveling up to her breasts, massaging them gently as his lips caressed along her neck. He removed one hand from under her shirt and slid the scrunchie from her hair, weaving his fingers in her tresses and as his kisses on her neck became more profound. The bulge on her backside throbbed against her, and she turned her head to kiss him erotically on his moist lips as ardent moans emerged from her mouth. After she turned around to him, he lifted her shirt over her head and unsnapped the front hook of her bra as her breasts bounced out. He took one hardened nipple in his mouth, sucking and tautening it as she ran her fingers through his curls.

His mouth moved to the other breast, sending heated pleasure through her veins and more amorous sounds from her. He trailed his hand to the button of her jeans and tugged her out of them, along with her tennis shoes. After picking her up, he set her on his bike, moving one of her hands to the handle and spread her legs as his tongue sank into her middle.

"Bryce..." she purred out as his tongue entered her. She laced her other hand in his hair so she wouldn't fall, even though he held her firmly by her bottom.

"You're too damn addictive," he said, twirling his tongue around her rosy bud. "I literally can't get enough of you."

Coiling his tongue around her opening, he glanced up with a lazy, sexy gaze. "I need to bottle your ambrosia into a liqueur and sell it. Make more millions." He dipped his tongue in and licked down the center of her lips. "But I don't like to share."

His possessive tone shook through her as she arched her back to consume more of his warmth.

"Stop talking," she demanded roughly, raking her hand through his curls and pushing him farther into her. Bryce continued licking and darting in and out as sensations rushed all over her trembling body. His wicked tongue kissed her other lips so passionately her legs began to shake uncontrollably. She longed to have him inside her, but she didn't want him to stop what he was doing, either.

Sydney let out a long groan as his tongue-action pace sped up, and her hips rose up and down while he tried to keep her still on the leather seat. An orgasm slammed through every inch of her as her body twisted, and he gathered her up in his arms and held her close to him. Once she calmed down, he lowered her back to the motorcycle and unzipped his pants, pulling them down along with his boxers. He grabbed the protection from his wallet and slipped it on before spreading her legs out again, this time resting one of them on the handle. He scooped up her butt a tad from the seat and entered her inch by magnificent inch until he was nestled deep inside her as he remained still.

"Don't drop me on the cement," she said seriously.

He leaned over and kissed her softly. "Trust me. I got you."

Sydney reached her hands up to his face as he slowly moved in and out of her with long, sensual thrusts. She didn't even know why she was concerned with him dropping her on the garage floor. She always felt completely safe with him.

His hands moved to her waist as he pulled her to him over and over, releasing earth-shattering sounds from her mouth. Sounds she didn't recognize as her own, but she didn't care as he continued stroking in and out, hitting her spot each time more and more aggressively. Powerful waves crashed through her, sending her on a blissful journey of freefalling. She no longer felt the firmness of the seat underneath. Just his strong hands guiding her back and forth to him.

"Who do you belong to?" he asked gruffly, lowering his head to hers.

"You, baby. Only you," she panted out against his lips.

He stopped for a moment, lifting her off the motorcycle, turning her around and bending her over as her feet stayed on the ground and legs shoulder width apart. In one thrust, he was snug inside her once more, taking his time moving to a steady rhythm. He pulled her against him as her muscles clenched around him, sending trembles to rippling through her. The man was deep in her body and her spirit. Yes, all of her belonged to him. Her heart and mind included. She'd never been so in sync with a man in all aspects of her life, but for the first time she was. And for the first time she knew she wanted to be with only him.

Bryce's vibrations began to speed up along with his thrusts as she held on to the handles of the motorcycle. His grunts and groans became more intense as did the orgasm that shook his body and then hers. He slumped over, being cautious not to smash her into the seat. He kissed the side of her neck and her cheek as he lifted her face to him.

"Who do you belong to again?" he asked, his eyes staring straight into her soul.

Sydney simply smiled.

She was falling in love with Bryce.

Chapter 12

"Wow, someone's on time for lunch," Megan said as Sydney and Tiffani arrived five minutes late at The Cheesecake Factory at Perimeter Mall for lunch. They'd scheduled a late lunch for three o'clock since Tiffani got off at 2:30 p.m. and worked at an elementary school around the corner from the restaurant. "You should take a vacation more often."

"Ha. Not funny, sissy," Sydney answered, giving her sister and cousin a hug.

The ladies sat down and skimmed through the menu. Once their orders were placed, they chatted about their day, with Sydney mostly listening or pretending to listen. Her thoughts tramped back to last night in the garage, afterward in front of the fireplace and this morning's breakfast in bed she made before Bryce left to head home and prepare for his busy day. This time when he kissed her goodbye, she didn't mention their Vegas agreement. She simply said, "I'll see you later."

"What do you think, Syd?" Megan asked.

Syd took a sip of her water. "About what?"

"What are you over there deep in thought about? I asked you about Tiffani's assorted cupcakes from the party." Megan stared at her with a weird expression, and Syd hoped her twin senses weren't kicking in.

"Oh, I thought the cupcake tier was a wonderful idea. It was very classy and elegant."

Tiffani's face beamed with appreciation. "Thank you. What were your favorite cupcakes?"

"I especially liked the turtle one and the coconut cream," she answered, deciding to rejoin the conversation. She was there to catch up with her family, not daydream about Bryce.

Megan gave her an odd looked with a swished lip. "I don't remember you having a turtle one," she announced. "I only packed up coconut cream cupcakes for you to take home."

And you're right, Syd thought. *I didn't, but Bryce did, and I could taste it when he kissed me in the bathroom.*

"No, I had one. Just didn't take any to go." Syd turned to her to cousin, hoping to steer the conversation away from how many cupcakes she did or didn't have. "So why did you call this special lunch, Tiffani?"

"Well," Tiffani started, "I have an announcement to make."

"We're all ears," Syd said, trying to avoid eye contact with Megan. She may not have been a profiler but because they had the same facial expressions and mannerisms, she could more often than not figure out what Syd was thinking.

Tiffani cleared her throat and smiled as her dimples indented. "As you know, I've baked a lot of different cupcakes for birthday parties, weddings and other events for the past few years for extra money since Keith died. I have a little of the insurance money left, and I've been saving in order to open a cupcake shop."

"Oh, that's wonderful!" Megan exclaimed, clapping. "Are you still going to teach?"

"No. I didn't sign my contract for the next school year. I hope to have the shop set up and running by this summer. I've found a few places not far from where I live, and KJ can still go to the same school where I teach since it's his home school. I've received so many orders lately, but it's time-consuming, especially with teaching and all of KJ's extracurricular activities. I have two orders this weekend for some of KJ's friends who are having birthday parties, and report cards go home next."

"Well, you've discussed this before when Keith was alive," Megan reminded her. "I supported you then and I support you now."

"Yes, but he didn't want me to start my own business, considering KJ was just a toddler. He preferred me to be a stay-at-home mother." Tiffani sighed with a wistful expression. "If it doesn't work out, I can always go back to teaching."

"That's wonderful you're following your dreams. Syd and I are very proud of you."

Syd chimed in. "Yes, we certainly are. If you need our help, just let us know."

"Oh, I will." Tiffani paused as the waitress arrived with their lunch. "And KJ is so excited. He's volunteered to be my accountant. I was, like, not yet, sweetie. He's so much like his father when it comes to money. I swear that little boy has more money under his bed in a shoe box than I do in my purse." Tiffani pulled her waist-length hair back into a ponytail before digging into her salad. "But I'm excited and Bryce has offered his real-estate agent to me so I'm really grateful for that."

"Oh, Bryce is helping you?" Megan asked with a lit-up face.

Sydney gulped. Was Megan still trying to set them up?

"I told him briefly about it at one of the tutorial sessions when I brought cupcakes for the children. He called the agent that helped him find an office building for his practice. I'm meeting with her to look at properties during Spring Break. I already have some in mind, though."

"But no sparks?" Megan questioned with a hopeful smile.

Sydney quietly continued to eat her grilled chicken salad as Tiffani laughed.

"He's definitely not my type. He's more your speed, Syd."

Syd nearly choked on a piece of lettuce. She grabbed

her water and took a sip, followed by a gulp. "Goodness, no."

"Don't worry. I wouldn't do that to either of you." Megan leaned back in her chair, sipping her tea. "Besides, you think Bryce is an ass, though he really isn't. But if he rubs you the wrong way, then I completely understand."

Syd's mind tramped back to all the times Bryce's hands rubbed her the right way. Tender. Rough. In between.

"Megan, why are you trying to set people up now? We tried setting you up, and you found your own man, a senator at that. I'm sure in due time Tiffani and I and even Bryce will be just as happy as you and Steven."

Megan twirled a shrimp around in her Alfredo sauce with a melancholy expression. "Oh, I know. I suppose you're right, but I overheard Steven and Bryce playing pool in the game room the night before last. Bryce said that he thinks he's in love and that it's someone he has known for a long time. He wouldn't tell Steven who. In fact, he said we would all be surprised. We suspect that it's Bryce's ex Linda, who lives in Savannah. She's been back and forth in town taking care of some family business, and I know he's seen her on one of her trips because he referred her mother to me. She's contemplating remodeling her kitchen and dining area. I met with them at the mother's fabulous home and while there, Bryce called Linda. You should've seen the way her face lit up, and she left the room for about twenty minutes. Mmm…maybe that's why he didn't ask Stephanie out.

Who knows? Y'all are right. I just want everyone to be happy like me and Steven."

Sydney sat numbly pretending to eat her salad as if she was uninterested in anything going on in Bryce's life. Except that wasn't the case. Was he trying to get back with his ex? She'd seen and spoken to him quite often since their return from Vegas. Even broken their agreement. Maybe she was getting her feelings caught up in something that wasn't real. Maybe she was wrong about her instinct with him, but she rarely was when it came to people. She was a profiler. She knew body language, reflections in voices and facial expressions. Nothing had seemed out of place, but she'd been wrong about him before. Was she still wrong but on a different level?

Tiffani left early to pick up KJ from his grandparents' and take him to swim lessons while Megan convinced her to window-shop in the mall.

"Syd?" Megan asked in a concerned tone.

Oh, boy. I know that tone.

"Yes?"

"There's something going on with you, but I can't pinpoint it." She stopped walking to gaze at a chair through the window before shaking her head and they continued past the store. "However, you've been different since you returned from Vegas…maybe even a little bit before."

"I just needed a vacation. I'd been working around the clock, but I think I know how to balance that now. A lot of the extra hours was me wanting to work overtime. I miss work, but it's good to not be there all the time, especially when I don't have to be."

"What about taking the bar? Is that something you're still considering?"

"I haven't thought about it anymore or even studied for it lately. At the end of the day, I love my career as a criminal profiler."

"I just want you to rest and eat properly," Megan said, squeezing her hand. "Whatever makes you happy I'm all for it."

"Awww…sissy." They stopped in the middle of the mall and gave each other a hug. "I love you."

"Love you, too." Megan pursed her lips together and slid her finger under Sydney's Pandora bracelet that she'd forgotten to take off. "I still think there's something you're not telling me, but I won't press the issue until you're ready to discuss it."

"Thank you. I sincerely appreciate that," she said. Sydney knew that Megan knew that she would've never bought the bracelet for herself.

She figured one day she would have to confide in her sister but not until she knew for certain what she and Bryce had was real.

Later on that evening, Sydney was hungry again, considering she only had a salad she had barely touched. She ventured out to The Iberian Pig, a Spanish and tapas restaurant in downtown Decatur that was a few blocks from her house. She had a craving for their braised veal ravioli and grilled pork tenderloins with Swiss chard.

She'd hoped to talk to Bryce just to hear his voice in her ear when she'd left the mall earlier, but he'd sent a text saying he was in meeting and had another one that evening. However, he said he'd call after his last meeting.

Sydney parallel parked her car across the street from the restaurant. She grabbed her purse from the passenger seat and rummaged around, looking for her cell phone. At first, she was going to eat at the restaurant. No big deal. She ate alone often. She wasn't one of those women who had to have a date or group of friends in order to eat out. But she decided to take her food to go as she fished around for her cell phone. She figured she'd just order and then pick it up inside. It shouldn't take longer than thirty minutes. In the meantime, she could walk around downtown. She had a lot on her mind that she needed to sort through and the cool March air would do her brain some good.

Megan's story about Bryce possibly still being in love with his ex didn't sit well with her even though they weren't in an official committed relationship. They were just friends with benefits, even though it didn't feel like it with him. She'd had relationships like that before, and that's all they were. But he made her feel real emotions that she hadn't experienced with any man. Not even her ex, who she had thought she was in love with. No, this was different. She'd fallen for the man who at one point she'd despised. Now she knew what a wonderful, caring person he was. He was kind-hearted, warm and giving. Yet Megan's words kept playing in her head, and she wanted to casually ask her again was she sure about his ex Linda. However, because no one knew about them, she couldn't. Megan would've found it odd that she would ask anything about Bryce. Plus, until she knew were they stood, she wasn't going to get carried away. Sydney was the logical, practical one. She always thought things through before making any rash decisions, especially with men. Suddenly, her thoughts were interrupted by a Mercedes that looked like Bryce's pulling up to a parking spot in front of the restaurant.

Her heart beat sped up when Bryce emerged, wearing a dashing smile, and walked around to the passenger side of the car. She slid down in her seat and glanced at the clock on the dashboard. It was seven o'clock on the dot. The time he mentioned for his business dinner. *Okay, he's just grabbing his briefcase. Darn it. Where are my binoculars when I need them? No big deal and I did tell him The Iberian Pig had excellent food.* Her heart stopped and then sank when he opened the door and a lady emerged. It was Stephanie, Megan's old friend from college.

Sydney pressed the button for the window and let it down a few inches so she could hear the conversation, but the cars passing by stopped any words from floating her way.

Stephanie placed her hand on Bryce's shoulder as she giggled about something he'd said. *Was it that funny? Probably not.* Syd had never cared for her in college because she was a big flirtatious tease, especially with the boys who came from privileged families. Now she had found the big prize. A Monroe man. They entered the restaurant laughing like two old friends as he held the door open for her, and she strolled in with a slight swish of the hips and a sexy glance over her shoulder.

Sydney didn't know what to think. She couldn't be mad because they'd never said they were in a relationship. They were supposed to end their tryst in Vegas, but that didn't happen. Now it would. She turned the ignition and headed home. Her stomach no longer felt empty. Now her heart was, but she couldn't be mad at him. She could only be mad at herself for thinking they had something more.

"Thank you again for picking me up," Stephanie said, getting out of Bryce's car in front of her apartment near Stone Mountain. He closed the door and walked with her to the edge of the sidewalk.

He pulled his coat to him. It was a chilly evening, but he knew where he would be warm and was itching to get there. "No problem. I'm glad I was able to pick you up on the way instead of you taking a cab or something."

"Well, the tow truck guy did offer to drop me off at the restaurant so I wouldn't miss my interview. I can't believe my starter just gave out." She extended her right hand, and he shook it firmly. "Thank you so much for the opportunity, Mr. Monroe."

"You're welcome," he said in the same professional tone he'd used all evening. "I have a few more candidates to interview for the position, but I'll have my assistant call you either way."

"No problem, and if you don't hire me—" she paused and stepped into his personal space, which he hated "—then we can always go on that date that Megan suggested."

He cleared his throat and stepped back. "Well, as flattering as that is, I'm seeing someone." He shoved his hands in his pockets.

She seemed taken aback and pursed her lips as if he was lying. "Interesting. Megan said you weren't."

"My sister-in-law doesn't need to know all of my business, but I am seeing someone." He had been thinking about Sydney all day, which was why he had selected a restaurant so close to her house. He was supposed to swing by after dinner, not drive to Stone Mountain. But he was a gentleman, and Stephanie was a friend of Megan's.

She smiled, tearing her eyes away from him. "Oh… well, this is awkward. I had an offer with Miles and Morris earlier today. I think I'll tell them yes in the morning. You don't need to have your assistant call me, either way."

He nodded. "It was a pleasure meeting you. Good luck with Miles and Morris. I'll see you in court, Counselor."

"You, too."

Bryce watched her walk up the sidewalk to her apartment before getting in his car and driving off back in the direction he'd just come. He breathed out a long sigh, glad the interview was over with. All Stephanie did was causally flirt and bat her long, fake eyelashes the entire time. He was simply doing a favor for Megan, hoping that her friend would be professional. However, with her experience and law background, she wouldn't have been a good fit for his practice. Turning onto interstate, he was relieved Stephanie decided to take a job offer somewhere else.

The drive to his original destination after the interview was less than twenty minutes now that rush hour traffic had ended. He pushed a button to let all four windows down to allow in some fresh air and push out Stephanie's perfume. It was too loud, like her makeup. He preferred Sydney's soft ambrosia scent and less-is-more approach to wearing makeup. He let the windows up and was glad the overkill smell was gone.

"Call Sydney," he said to his car's hands-free system.

Her phone rang through his speakers as he neared the interstate junction that would take him to her home.

"Hello?" she answered in a curt tone.

"Hey, Syd. I'm done with my meeting. I'm not far from you. Is it okay that I stop by?"

"No, not tonight," she answered in a cool, even tone.

"Are you all right? You don't sound well."

"I'm fine. I just don't think you should come over tonight or any other night."

"What?" He clenched his jaw and had to slow down a bit.

"You heard me. I think it's best that we stop sleeping together. It's not going anywhere, and there's no need to waste each other's time."

"Syd, I wasn't wasting my time with you. I like you. A lot," he said sincerely.

"I'm sure you do for sex purposes. Don't get me wrong, I've enjoyed our time together. I needed an outlet. Plus, it's been a while since I've had sex, and you definitely put out the drought. However, we can't continue like this, and I think it's best to stop before one of us gets too caught up. Besides, we're single. We may meet someone and end up really liking that person and want to go out with him or her. You know, someone to laugh at your corny jokes. Can't be in a friends-with-benefits kinda relationship, or at least I can't. I'm not that type of woman. So it's best to end this now."

"Sydney, I'm not seeing anyone but you."

"Mmm…maybe not yet, but you will eventually."

"I don't think you understand, babe. I only want to be with you."

She laughed sarcastically. "Bryce, stop. Just stop. Okay? Don't dig a hole for yourself."

As he approached the fork in the road, he knew he had to make a decision. "Syd, how about I drop by, and we can discuss this in person." He slowed down to wait for her answer.

"Please don't. I gotta go. Take care."

The buzzing of the phone remained in his speakers,

and he drove like that halfway home until the computerized operator told him to hang up and please place his call again. He pushed the button on the steering wheel to end the call.

He honestly didn't know what had happened, but it didn't mean he was going to let her go so easily.

Chapter 13

Syd sat at her desk on her first official day back from her vacation, studying pictures of different crime scenes over the course of three years from possibly the same serial killer. She was looking for similarities in each while waiting for DNA samples to come in, but her thoughts kept shifting to Bryce. It had been over a week since their last conversation after she'd spotted him with Stephanie. He hadn't called back or shown up, and she was glad he hadn't. He'd become her weakness. To see Bryce would be to crave him, which was why she hadn't wanted him to come over that evening. She knew he'd play attorney, giving her evidence A through Z on why they should continue whatever it was they were doing.

A tap on her ajar door pulled her from thoughts of being in the warmth of Bryce's arms again. She immediately pushed her thoughts aside when she saw Mumford standing there with his glasses on his nose and his blue eyes peering over them.

"Chase, welcome back. I'm surprised you weren't here at seven o'clock this morning."

"Nope, I've decided since my schedule says nine to five. I'm going to try my best to follow that unless it's a drastic situation."

He strode in with his coffee and sat in the chair in front of her desk, nodding his head. "Vacation finally opened your eyes that you needed to relax, huh?"

She took her reading glasses off. "Yep."

"You had fun?"

She thought about all the fun she'd had, mostly with Bryce. "I'll say. I had a blast but now it's time to get back to reality and my life as I know it—without the extra hours at work, of course."

"Good. You know you have two more weeks saved up."

"I know. I'll take one this summer and one in the fall or winter." She'd already started making plans for a five-day Caribbean cruise for that summer.

"Great." He rose and checked his watch. "Debriefing in thirty minutes."

"I'll be there. Oh, and I brought some fresh fruit. It's in the break room."

He stopped and turned back around. "So you're the one who brought the fresh fruit? Hmm...well, I did have an apple even though I was looking for a doughnut."

"Well, an apple a day keeps the doctor away."

"Yep, and so does the baby aspirin I take once a day, but I'll add the apple just for you, Syd."

"Thank you, old man," she said with a sincere smile.

"Great to have you back. See you in a few," he said, closing her door all the way shut as her cell phone rang.

Pushing aside the gory files on her desk, Syd grabbed her phone and saw her sister's face on the screen.

"Hey."

"Hello, Syd. I wanted to make sure you were still coming to Savannah this weekend for the ribbon cutting of the Claire Monroe Community Center."

Sydney had forgotten all about that. She'd agreed to go but that was before she'd ended her affair with Bryce. She wasn't ready to see him so soon yet. She thought by the time the summer rolled around with family cookouts and other events she'd be long over him.

"Oh…thank you for the reminder." *But how can I get out of this?*

"Remember to stop by Tiffani's house to bring the cupcakes since she isn't able to make it. What time are you leaving again on Saturday morning?"

Guess I'm going. "After I pick up the cupcakes."

"Perfect. Thank you so much for doing this for me. I'll be flying in from Destin, Florida, late Friday night. We're decorating a beach house for the summer edition for the show."

"No problem, sis. So who all's coming to the ribbon cutting and the cocktail party at the Monroe family home?" The Monroe family home was where the Monroe children grew up until they'd moved to Atlanta. The house—located in the historical district of Savannah—was now owned by Bryce and Steven.

"Let's see. You. Me and Steven. His parents. Some business associates. Honestly, no one we really know, so you can keep me company. Oh, and I'm making sure your favorite room that faces the park with the Jack and Jill bathroom is ready, but you don't have to share it with anyone since Tiffani isn't coming. His parents have the master on the main since his father sprained his ankle playing golf. Steven and I are in the in-law suite upstairs."

"What about Bryce?"

"He's not attending even though he did donate half the money for it, but he just told me a few minutes ago he couldn't make it. Work-related things with the new practice opening soon and what not. Plus, Bryce doesn't like being in the limelight. He just wants the children to have a safe place to go after school and during the summer."

Syd exhaled and swirled her chair around. "How nice." *Yes, how nice indeed.*

"Oh…and wear that straight black dress with the spaghetti straps. You know, the one you wore to my engagement party."

"Megan…"

"It's an after-five affair. The men will be in tuxedos."

"Oh. Just checking. No more blind dates!" she warned.

"Now you know how I felt," Megan said teasingly.

They said their goodbyes, and Sydney headed off

to her debriefing, glad that Bryce wouldn't be at the ribbon cutting this weekend even though a part of her was sort of disappointed. However, she was just having withdrawals and in time she'd be fine. She couldn't believe that at one point she'd actually thought she'd fallen in love with Bryce. The idea was totally absurd.

Saturday morning, Sydney headed to the Steven R. Monroe Community Center in Atlanta to pick up the cupcakes from Tiffani. The last place she wanted to meet her was there, but Syd had overslept and Tiffani needed to be at the center by 7:45 a.m. to set up for the tutorial workshop. The cupcakes were already packed, so all she had to do was transfer them from Tiffani's backseat to hers and be on her way without running into Bryce.

When Syd pulled up, she parked next to her cousin's car and sent a short text for Tiffani to come outside with the keys. Syd got out and leaned on her car. She saw Bryce's motorcycle—the one they'd made love on—parked right outside the door. She sighed as she remembered that day. He'd held her and looked at her as if she was the only girl in the world for him, but she knew that wasn't the case, and she was fine with that. At least that's what she told herself. Last night, she'd barely slept thanks to him showing up in her dreams and taking her on a late-night motorcycle rendezvous and making love in front of the fireplace with rose petals scattered about.

Her eyes and thoughts shifted as the double doors of

the center opened. Her breathing became unhinged as Bryce strolled out with Tiffani's keys. He was ruggedly handsome in a pair of khakis and a black golf shirt that showcased his muscular arms. Arms she missed being snuggled in. His goatee was neatly trimmed around his yummy lips. Lips she yearned to feel on every inch of her skin just one more time.

"Good morning," he said in his deep baritone voice, pressing the remote twice to unlock the back door of Tiffani's Honda. "Push the driver seat down so I can slide the cooler on your backseat."

"Okay," she answered quietly, doing as he asked and stepping out of the way so he could place the container in her car.

He pushed the seat back and held her door open. "So you're going to the ribbon cutting of the new center in Savannah, huh?"

"Yes, and I'm running late," she answered, getting into the car and trying her best not to make eye contact with him. His smoldering gaze was on her, and every part of her being wanted and needed to kiss him. "So I may miss that depending on traffic, but I'll be at the cocktail party tonight at the Monroe family home." She started her Mustang but couldn't close the door because he was holding on to it. She caught a glimpse of herself in the rearview mirror. She was still wearing her hair wrap. *How freakin wonderful! If I'm going to see him, I should at least look incredible and not like I just rolled out of bed. Which I just did in his darn sweatpants. Great. Just great!*

"Cool. I grew up in that house. You've been before?"

"Just once with Megan right after her engagement. We stayed in the rooms with the Jack and Jill bathroom. She said they were yours and Steven's childhood rooms."

"Yes. Steven's old room faces the park and mine faces the backyard," he answered, glancing down at the sweats she wore, raising a curious eyebrow along with an arrogant curved grin. "Well…I won't hold you up. Have a safe trip."

"Thank you."

His dark stare lingered on hers for a second longer before closing the door.

Bryce entered the community center's gym, his eyes scanning the large facility as he ignored a few reporters who wanted an interview with him. He instructed them to speak with Senator Steven Monroe or former senator Robert Monroe, his father. He moved through the crowd of people, nodding and shaking a few hands as he straightened his designer tie under his gray suit jacket. He caught the attention of his mother, who strode his way with a pleasantly surprised smile on her lovely sienna face. Her thick gray hair was pulled back into a neat bun, which accentuated the Tiffany pearl necklace and matching bracelet he'd given to her last Mother's Day. She was an elegant and graceful woman who loved nice yet simple things.

"What are you doing here?" Claire Monroe asked.

"I thought you couldn't make it, or rather, didn't want to make it."

He smiled sheepishly. "Never said I didn't want to come. I just have a lot on my plate with the opening of my practice. However, Steven called and asked me one more time this morning. So after the tutorial session, I drove home, grabbed a few things and here I am."

"How did you get here? You didn't drive one of those fast motorcycles, did you?" She pinched his arm playfully.

"No, Mother. The private jet. I'd still be on the road if I'd driven."

"Well, you missed the ribbon-cutting ceremony and we only have about one more hour here, but I know you don't care about that." She patted his face and smiled warmly. "Your father is around here somewhere with Steven talking to the press. I'm going to go join the twins in the classroom section."

"I'll escort you." He held out his arm, and she slid her hand through it.

"Always such the gentleman. You're going to make someone a lucky lady one day."

Bryce smiled. He was working on it and was sure his mother would love her considering she loved Megan like her own daughter and was fond of Sydney, as well. His mother always said she liked Syd's spunkiness. He did, too.

He'd missed her. Missed her a lot. When their eyes had met that morning, it had taken everything in him not to grab her and shower her with kisses and hold her close to him. He wasn't sure what had happened to make her not want to see him anymore. He just hoped she realized that as long as their family had events, she'd have to face him whether she wanted to or not.

When Steven had called earlier that morning, Bryce wasn't aware that Sydney was going until Tiffani mentioned Sydney was taking cupcakes. He'd thought about telling Syd he'd see her there but decided against it. At first, he had no interest in going but seeing her in his sweatpants and wearing the bracelet he'd given her gave him some hope that she cared for him more than she realized.

When he entered the classroom with his mother, his eyes zoomed in on Sydney as she spoke with a family about the programs offered at the center. He was quite impressed by her knowledge as she spoke very eloquently and answered the parents' questions. She glanced for a second in his direction, and the blaze he knew all too well flashed for a moment. But she never missed a beat of her conversation or lost her poise.

Claire left his side and stood with Megan while she conversed with a mother and her young son. Bryce leaned against the wall and raked his eyes slowly over Sydney. Her hair was styled in the cute fluffy bob cut with an extra flounce to it, minimal makeup—not that she needed any—and a smart straight black pencil skirt and a ruffled teal blouse. On her wrist was the bracelet. For the first time he noticed a third charm, but he couldn't make out what it was.

Once Megan was done, she approached him with

her long hair bouncing around her shoulders, wearing a straight purple sheath dress with a black belt clinched at the waist.

"Hey there," she said, giving him a hug and kiss on the cheek. "I was shocked when Steven said you were coming, but so happy you did. It's because of you that the center is being opened in your mother's childhood neighborhood."

"Thank you, Megan, but you know I don't care about accolades. So what's next on the agenda? I'm sure you and my mom have a weekend of events planned for the family."

"You know us so well," his mother said, intertwining her arm with Megan's. "We're headed back to the house soon to relax. The party starts at six and then tomorrow a farewell brunch. Are you staying that long or headed back tonight?"

He glanced at Sydney, who had walked over and stood on the other side of his mother since the family she was speaking to had left. His mother intertwined her other arm through Sydney's and looked at her warmly.

"Yep. I'll be here all weekend," he said, flashing a gracious smile. He followed the ladies out of the classroom and was finally able to get a look at the third charm on Syd's bracelet. It read Vegas.

He'd learned long ago from his mother that women were sentimental. They kept things that were near and dear to them otherwise they'd toss or misplace them. They also bought and collected items that reminded them of something or someone special. His mother had a collection of Eiffel Tower items because his father had proposed to her at the top of it. She also saved all the homemade cards from her children in a keepsake trunk.

Bryce took note of the third charm. He could've been overthinking it, but Sydney wasn't the type to just buy something, especially a piece of jewelry for she rarely wore it.

Now he was elated that he'd changed his mind about coming to Savannah for the weekend. And by the end of it, he would convince Sydney that they belonged together.

Chapter 14

"Megan, I can't do that!"

Sydney was in her room at the Monroe family home in a frantic state at the audacity of the words that had just spewed from her sister's mouth. They'd just returned from the community center and had a few more hours before the cocktail party started.

"Syd, I know you can't stand him, but this is his home and that is his room," Megan pointed out. "I have no place else to put him. You only have to share the shower area. You each have your own vanity room that has a door that locks. Just lock the door," she said in a calm tone.

Syd washed her hands over her face and sighed as she thought about the last time she'd shared a shower with Bryce. *Literally.*

"Isn't there another bedroom with its own bathroom connected? You showed it to me last time we were here."

"Yes, but it's still completely empty as far as furniture. Just a bunch of boxes."

"I'll use that bathroom."

"Fine," Megan said, heading to the door. "I'm going to go check on things downstairs and then take a short nap before the guests arrive." Megan gave her a thoughtful smile before closing the door.

Sydney sat on the window seat with the oversize comfy pillows and looked out at the park across the street, where children were playing as their mothers watched and chatted. She couldn't believe Bryce had shown up unannounced and now he was going to occupy his childhood bedroom just on the other side of the shared bathroom. Yes, she knew that this was his house, but if she'd known he was coming, she would've stayed at one of the bed-and-breakfasts nearby or made up some excuse to leave right after the ribbon cutting, such as a big case, and jetted back to Atlanta.

She watched the cars go by on the street and wondered how the heck all of this started. If only she hadn't passed out at work. If only she'd hadn't called Megan, then she wouldn't have in turned called Bryce and that delicious kiss would've never happened. But she also wouldn't have had the best month of her life.

A motorcycle slowing down in front of the house caught her attention, and she recognized the helmet and the bike. The last time Syd was there with Megan, she'd seen it in the garage along with a few luxury cars that were housed there for whenever someone from the Monroe family needed a car to drive.

Bryce took off his helmet and looked up when he saw her perched on the window seat. He winked, flashing a million-dollar smile. She turned away from the window with a groan and closed the drapes.

She flew over to the vanity room door that led to the shared shower area and locked it and then lay across the bed. She was tired from last night's tossing and turning, and she had a feeling she would be again tonight with Bryce in the next bedroom over. She held on to her pillow and drifted off to sleep with thoughts of him etched into her brain.

Sydney woke up to the alarm on her cell phone an hour and a half later. She stretched and yawned, feeling refreshed. It was a little bit before five so she padded across the room to the vanity area and water running in the bathroom. The fresh scent of soap awakened her even more, and part of her wanted to go in there and join him under the water as they had done in Vegas.

She decided she would skip down the hall to the other bathroom and take a quick shower. Even though she really didn't want to. She'd taken a shower in the shared bathroom before going to the community center, and the waterfall showerhead was the best shower she'd ever taken—next to the one with Bryce. The running water stopped, and she froze. The rings of the shower curtain skidded back across the rod, and he cleared his throat. She quietly gathered her toiletries and almost cursed at herself when she remembered the only gel she'd brought was in the room where he was along with the linen closet.

She listened for him to leave so she could skedaddle in there, grab it and a towel and be on her way to the other bathroom. A light knock on the door next to her interrupted her thoughts, startling her.

"Yes?" she asked quietly. *How did he know I was standing here?*

"I'm done," he said in his deep voice she loved to hear in her ear.

"Okay."

"You know you can shower in here. I promise to give you your privacy despite the fact I've seen every single sexy inch of you."

"Shh…"

"No one can hear us, Sydney."

"Why didn't you tell me this morning you were coming?"

"Are we going to continue to talk through the door?"

"Are you dressed?"

"If you count this towel wrapped around my waist as dressed, then sure."

She opened the door slowly to see him standing there fine and glistening with the towel wrapped around him; however, it was doing nothing to hide the slight erection that had formed. She strained to keep her eyes on his face and not his provoking wet chest. That wasn't a great idea, either, because of the intense way he stared at her as his jaw twitched. It was the same gaze he'd given her the last time they were in a bathroom together at Megan and Steven's home. She stepped back out of his personal space and tried to divert her eyes away from his manly physique before she reached out and slid her hand along his abs.

A glimmer formed in his eyes, but he didn't move.

"So answer my question," she said, folding her arms across her chest to stop the fantasy in her head.

"If we were still speaking, you would've known I was coming. It was a last-minute thing. Steven asked me, and since I believe in family first, here I am. I'm going to get dressed. I have to be down early, according to my mother. Enjoy your shower, and I promise not to disturb you."

He pivoted on his heel and went out the opposite door that led to his vanity area. He closed the door and locked it from his side.

Breathing a sigh of relief, she took a quick shower and then bolted back to her side, making sure to lock her door even though she trusted he wouldn't barge in.

An hour later, she emerged downstairs at the party. Guests had begun to arrive as the waitstaff carried hors d'oeuvres and champagne on trays. Megan was being the gracious hostess she always was along with Ms. Claire, as Sydney called her. The men, mostly friends of Mr. Monroe, were clad in tuxedos and sipping on drinks. The women had on fabulous cocktail and after-five dresses. Her gaze caught Bryce's for a moment as a woman approached him and gave him a big hug. She beamed from ear to ear and even slid her hand down his face before letting him go.

"Hey," Megan said, handing her a glass of champagne. "I was looking for you."

"Just made it down. Everything looks really nice." Sydney glanced around the room, trying not to focus on Bryce. "Who's the young lady with Bryce? She looks familiar." Sydney lied. She'd never seen her before in her life and if she hadn't left her cell phone upstairs, she could've done facial recognition and a background check all within five minutes or less.

"Oh, that's his ex Linda that I was telling you and Tiffani about. She's definitely smitten with him—that's for sure. But enough about them." Megan pulled her by the hand out onto the veranda. "I have someone I want to you to meet."

"Huh?" Sydney asked in disbelief, taking a sip of her champagne.

"Oh…it's not a blind date. If you don't like him, there's another guy I want you to meet."

They approached an extremely handsome man with butterscotch skin, a bald head and a goatee that was not as alluring as Bryce's. He had a pleasant demeanor and looked hot in a tuxedo. He was definitely a tall glass of water and with a beautiful smile, yet not a single emotion stirred in her.

"Scott Banks, this is my twin sister I was telling you about, Sydney. Syd, Scott is contemplating running for one of the congressional seats in Georgia in the upcoming election and Steven is mentoring—"

"Excuse me, Mrs. Monroe, can you tell me how you want the cupcakes set and where?" Greta Reid, the Monroes' head housekeeper, asked.

"Sure, I'll be right there," Megan answered, before turning back to Sydney, who was fuming on the inside. "You two just hang out and get to know each other." Megan hurried back inside with Greta.

Scott chuckled. "So I guess Megan is trying to set us up?"

"Yep. She certainly is." Sydney through clenched teeth.

"Well…I definitely don't mind." His eyes traveled over her, then settled on her face. "You're a very beautiful woman. Steven and Megan have both spoken highly of you."

Sydney nodded as she saw Bryce and Linda pass by the window. He looked outside and raised an eyebrow as his forehead lines formed.

Sydney touched her face and frowned. "This south Georgia weather is a little muggy. Can we go inside and chat? Grab something cool to drink?"

"Of course," he said, holding out his arm as she intertwined her hand around the bend of his elbow.

For the rest of the evening, Sydney hung out with Scott, as well as mingling with the other guests. However, neither her thoughts nor her eyes could stay away from Bryce and Linda, who followed him around like a puppy dog. She was a cute girl, Syd supposed. Curvy body that looked as if she turned down food as opposed to working out and staying fit. She had way too many extensions on her head and her oversize jewelry was just plain gaudy.

Sydney didn't see how Linda could've ever been his type. She was too prissy and way too picky. When the waiter asked her if she wanted a stuffed blue cheese tomato, she wrinkled her nose in protest. Sydney was relieved when Scott was pulled away by some of his father's colleagues to discuss his upcoming campaign. Syd grabbed a few shrimp puffs from a tray passing by and retreated back outside onto the veranda. She wasn't sure where Bryce had disappeared to, and in a way she didn't care. At least she kept telling herself that. She knew in her heart she was in love with him, and it wasn't because she saw him with Linda or even Stephanie. She knew long before then. Long before he'd ever kissed her in the hospital.

The sliding glass door of the veranda squeaked, and she looked up to see Megan approach with a plate of food and a glass of champagne. She set all of it on the table in front of the couch.

"So glad it's almost over with," Megan said, crashing next to Sydney.

"Really? Because I'm so ready to retreat to my room."

"Yep. Everyone is pretty much leaving. Scott was looking for you, but his brother was ready to go, so he left me his card to give you."

Sydney shrugged. "Not interested." She sighed and grabbed Megan's champagne glass and took a sip.

"What's wrong? And don't tell me nothing," Megan

stated in her mother hen, concerned tone. "You've been acting really weird lately."

Sydney sighed and spilled everything to Megan about her and Bryce, from the kiss in the hospital to their encounter that morning when she'd picked up the cupcakes, as her sister stared in disbelief with saucer-shaped eyes and her mouth hanging to her lap.

Megan placed her hands over her mouth and shook her head. "You and Bryce? Never in a million years would I ever have expected that you and him would ever hook up!"

"Me, either."

"I knew something was up with you lately, but Bryce never crossed my mind. I thought maybe you were seeing someone at work, like that Watkins guy or an ex or someone else, but never Bryce." She laughed uncontrollably, taking a swig of her champagne.

"Well, now I know why you were adamant about not wanting to share a bathroom with him. Even though I'm still in shock you fell in love with the man you've despised for years. Does Bryce know how you feel?"

"No, and it doesn't matter." Sydney leaned back on the couch and closed her eyes, trying to suppress the tears that wanted to fall. "Isn't he trying to get back with Linda?"

Megan bit into a cupcake. "Mmm…I don't know. They've been together for the majority of the evening. Then again, Steven invited her when he confirmed that Bryce was coming, so it's not like he invited her. She just received a big promotion at the Fortune 500 company she works for, so I doubt she's trying to move to Atlanta to be with Bryce. She was only in Atlanta helping her parents with some medical concerns."

"I've decided not to worry about it. It was fun while it lasted, and at least I learned that Bryce isn't such a bad guy after all." Sydney stood, grabbing a stuffed tomato from her sister's plate and popping it into her mouth. "Just please keep this between us and please stop setting me up on blind dates. Now I know what you felt like a few years ago. And then you went out and found your own man."

Megan shrugged with a smirk. "Something like that. And maybe you have, as well."

Sydney laughed sarcastically. "Good night. See you at brunch."

She made her way up the stairs finally after bidding a few of the guests who were leaving good-night and going to the kitchen to make a big plate of leftovers before the caterers packed everything up. She still hadn't seen Bryce, but she figured he was off somewhere with his ex. She threw off her clothes and slipped into her pajamas and grabbed some of the photo albums that were in the room on a bookshelf. They were filled with Monroe family vacations throughout the years in their Winnebago or on a yacht. Bryce had indeed grown into a handsome, charismatic man from the scrawny little boy she saw in the pictures. By high school he began to fill out with a few whiskers under his nose, and by senior year, he was the star basketball player and senior class president.

She closed the book when a light tap on the bathroom door startled her. Glancing at the clock on the nightstand, she saw it was just a little after midnight. Reluctantly, she strolled toward the door and opened it to find Bryce wearing jeans and a leather jacket over a sweater. He held a pink motorcycle helmet in one hand and a black one in the other. His eyes glanced over her pajamas.

"Change clothes," he demanded in a deep voice, handing her the pink helmet. "We're going for a ride."

"It's midnight," she said, handing the helmet back to him, but he didn't take it.

"I'm driving," he answered, walking toward the door of her room.

"That's not—"

"Get dressed and meet me out front in five minutes."

After he left, she tossed off her pajamas, threw on a pair of jeans and a sweater. Grabbing the helmet and her jacket, she peeked out the door first, then closed it gently. The house was quiet, and she made it out the front door without being noticed.

Bryce was already on the motorcycle waiting for her. She hopped on and barely had her arms wrapped around him before he took off.

Leaving the residential area, he turned on a back country road and sped up, much to her dismay. Not a car in sight but that didn't mean he had to speed like he owned the street. She wasn't sure how long they'd driven, but she guessed about an hour, especially when she saw a sign that read Welcome to South Carolina. He finally stopped in front of a gate and pulled a remote from his pocket and pushed a button on it. The gate opened, and he zoomed in and drove for what seemed another mile as beach sand appeared on both sides of the road. He pulled up in front of a house and continued on until he reached the edge of the driveway. He stopped abruptly, and she jumped off.

She walked away from him, then turned back around and raised the visor of her helmet. "Why the heck were you driving so fast?" she yelled at the top of her lungs.

"Because I needed to," he said calmly, getting off the motorcycle but not following her.

She continued walking until her boots were in the pillowy beach sand.

"Where are we, and what are we doing here?" she shouted. She was still furious about how fast he was driving. He knew she hated that.

"Monroe Beach Villa, right outside of Hilton Head, and we're here to talk."

"We couldn't do that in Savannah at your other house?"

"Follow me."

Moments later, they entered the vast foyer with a tiled floor that continued on to the kitchen. She followed him through to the living room that contained oversize white couches with teal toss pillows. High wood-beamed ceilings and walnut hardwood floors made it the perfect beach getaway. But she wasn't there to admire the decor.

She sat down in one of the chairs and placed her helmet on the carved-wood table in front of her.

"So what are we talking about?" She crossed her legs and looked up at him, since he was still standing with a smug look on his face.

"The fact that you just wanted to all of a sudden stop seeing each other without any valid explanation."

Taken aback, she stood directly in front of him. "No! I gave you a very valid explanation. If one of us started seeing someone else and it got serious, then we would have to end what we're doing. I just thought it would be best to end it now before one of us…" Her voice trailed off as her mind took her back to seeing him with Stephanie.

"What?" he yelled. "One of us what, Syd?"

She sighed and stepped back. "Fell for the other person and then wound up hurt when there was someone else in the picture."

"But I told you on the phone that night I only wanted to be with you. That's it, Syd. I want to explore a relationship with you and only you."

She laughed sarcastically and stared up at him with a raised eyebrow. "What about Stephanie?"

"Your sister set that up. Trust me—I don't like Stephanie."

"Really? Megan set up the date at The Iberian Pig?"

He frowned with confusion and shook his head. "How did you know about The Iberian Pig?"

"Because I saw you and her getting out of the car laughing and what not," she said, pointing her finger at his chest. "You know if you're going to date, fine. But must you do it in my neighborhood? Hell, I'm the one who told you about the restaurant in the first place." Sydney stormed to the other side of the room, turning away from him.

"So you're spying on me? Got some type of tracking device on my phone or my car, Agent Chase?"

She turned to face him with anger rising from here. "No, idiot! Not spying on you. I went to grab some dinner and I saw you, and then you had the audacity to want to come over afterward? What? Stuck-up tease Stephanie wouldn't give you any, so you called me?"

"Are you through fussing or are you going to continue until you pop a blood vessel on the side of your beautiful neck?" he asked calmly, sitting on the couch and crossing his foot up on his opposite knee. "I mean, you are sexy when you're mad, so go ahead and get it all out. Just let me know when it's my turn."

"Oh, I'm done," she said, standing over him. "So done." She sat back in the chair and stared him down. "Say what you gotta say, and then I'm leaving."

He tried to muffle a laugh. "How do you plan on leaving?"

"All the Monroe vacation homes have a car or two in the garage."

"Oh…so you're going to steal my Lexus?"

She groaned. "Please say what you need to say," she said through clenched teeth.

"Fine." He stood, pacing back and forth as if he

were in the courtroom ready to give closing arguments. "Make sure to put on your profiler thinking cap."

She sighed and rolled her eyes. "This is not the court-house."

"First of all, your sister introduced me to Stephanie with the hopes of some type of love connection. How-ever, that wasn't going to happen. For two reasons. One of which, she isn't my type, but she's an attorney looking for a job, so I offered her a chance for an interview. However, she wasn't able to make it at the time I suggested dur-ing lunch hours because she had a few more interviews that day. Since she's a friend of yours and Megan's—"

"Just Megan," she reminded him. "We were never friends."

He cleared his throat. "Anyway, I offered a dinner in-terview instead and told her The Iberian Pig was supposed to be a great place. On my way, she called and said her car broke down a few blocks away and she was running late. I went to where she was with the tow truck, and, instead of canceling, we went ahead and had the interview over din-ner, where apparently you saw us getting out of the car."

"Really? Interview? You opened her door. Sounds like a date to me."

"My mother raised me to be a gentleman."

"Did you offer her a job?"

"Nope. Never got the chance to. In fact, wasn't going to. She wouldn't represent my firm well. Plus..." He hesitated and twisted his lip. "She asked me out when I dropped her off."

"Oh, I'm not surprised at all. She hasn't changed

since college. She loves latching on to men with loads of money."

He nodded with a knowing smirk. "Yes, I sensed that, but I told her no because I was seeing someone. At least I thought I was, until you told me otherwise, despite me telling you that I only want to be with you."

She exhaled at his words. She wanted so badly to believe him and so far she did, but she still needed to resolve one more issue.

"What about Linda?"

He wrinkled his entire face, and Sydney took note of that expression.

"Linda is my ex from undergrad. We dated about one semester, but trust me, she isn't interested in me. Not at all."

"She was all over you tonight."

"Like you were all over her ex Scott Banks?" he asked matter-of-factly, rubbing his goatee.

"Ex?" she asked, barely above a whisper.

"Yes, she was trying to make him jealous. She told me beforehand when she found out he would be there after Steven invited her. For some reason, my big brother thought I was talking about her a few weeks ago when I told him I'd fallen in love with someone. She'd been in town helping her parents with some things and I referred her mom to Megan for some kitchen renovations. Linda and I have always been cool because we didn't have that serious of a relationship in college."

"Oh…"

"Of course, I didn't expect to see you there with Scott

trying to make me jealous. I almost wanted to punch old boy out. Except he's a cool dude. Apparently, they'd had some type of argument and broke up a month or so ago. However, I think they'll get back together. Neither of them enjoyed seeing the other with someone else. You know what I mean, Syd?"

"Oh." Sydney didn't know what else to say as she listened to Bryce. She knew in her heart he was telling the truth, and now she risked the chance of losing him forever if she didn't say something.

"Bryce…I…"

"Look, let me make this clear to you, Sydney Michelle Chase." He pulled her up and held her by the waist, wearing a stern expression. "I never go into this much detail explaining myself to a woman, but I love *you* and I only want to be with you."

Tears welled in her eyes, and she shook her head in disbelief. "Wait…" She paused, placing her hand on his chest and staring up at him as a tear fell down her cheek. He wiped it away. "Say that again."

He bent down to her height and set his hands on either side of her face. "I said I love you." He kissed her forehead, her cheeks and her lips gently.

"I love you, too, Bryce. Very, very much."

He picked her up and twirled her around before lifting her totally up and carrying her upstairs to the bedroom.

A few hours later, they lay naked on top of the sheets, their legs and arms intertwined together after a few lovemaking sessions.

"Our families are going to be so surprised when we tell them we're together," she said, resting her chin on his chest and looking up at him. "Well…I told Megan tonight that I was in love with you. Of course, she was ecstatic."

"I'm sure she was, and I told Steven tonight, as well, after the cocktail party. He told me don't be stupid and let you get away."

She laughed and sat up to straddle him. He wrapped his hands around her waist. "I'm not going anywhere, Counselor." She leaned down and kissed him softly. But then he pulled her down farther and kissed her profoundly, causing the tingles only he could create to rush through her. She so loved the feeling and him even more.

"So I have you for life, Agent Chase?"

"Are you proposing?" she asked with a wide smile.

"Yes. Will you marry me and spend the rest of your life being the little spitfire I fell for five years ago?"

She laughed as joyous tears rolled down her cheeks. "Yes. I can do that."

He flipped her over and they made love again with Sydney laughing and crying the entire time. She was so happy to finally be with the man she hadn't even re- alized she'd loved for a very long time.

The next morning, Bryce brought her coffee to the bed before they were to head back to Savannah for the farewell brunch and announce their news to every- one. He sat on the edge of the bed while she sipped her coffee, the sunshine beaming through the blinds. For some reason, now that she was with Bryce, she loved the early-morning sun with her coffee, especially if he made it.

He kissed her cheek and pulled her onto his lap. "Tomorrow, we're going to fly to New York City and I'm taking you to Tiffany and Co. so you can pick out your engagement ring. And if you want, you can stand outside the store and eat pastries and sip coffee like Audrey Hepburn did in your favorite movie."

"Aww…that's the sweetest thing you've ever said to me. I'd love to." She kissed him tenderly. "I love you, Bryce."

"And I love you, Sydney and I look forward to the new journey we've embarked on."

* * * * *

REQUEST YOUR FREE BOOKS!

2 FREE NOVELS
PLUS 2 FREE GIFTS!

KIMANI™
ROMANCE

Love's ultimate destination!

 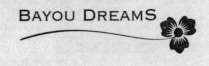

She was well
worth the wait…

Thief OF MY *Heart*

JANICE SIMS

Psychologist Desiree Gaines diagnosed Decker Riley the day they
met: he's a sexy smooth-talker who loves the thrill of the chase. But
for the first time since she lost her fiancé, Desiree is intrigued. When
Desiree finally steps into his arms, he realizes she was meant to be
with him. But Decker's past makes Desiree doubt herself, so he'll
have to earn her trust, one sweet, sizzling kiss at a time…

KIMANI
HOTTIES
FOREVER MY LADY

"Sexy and exciting, this story will keep you on the edge of your seat
from start to finish." —*RT Book Reviews* on *SAFE IN MY ARMS*

HARLEQUIN®
™ www.Harlequin.com

Available February 2015
wherever books are sold!